Sreedhevi Iyer

Jungle Without Water
AND OTHER STORIES

London
*Jet*stone
2017

A *Jetstone* paperback original.

ISBN 9781910858103

The right of Sreedhevi Iyer to be identified as
author in this work has been asserted in accordance
with the Copyright, Designs and Patents Act, 1988.

Cover design by The Ever Shifting Subject.

Contents

For my parents

Acknowledgments

"Green Grass" first appeared in *Drunken Boat*, Issue 14, 2011.

"Cake and Green M&Ms" originally appeared in *DotLit*, Vol. 5, No. 1, 2005.

"Circular Feed" was first published in *Asia Literary Review* 31, 2016.

A different version of "I.C." was anthologised in *Everything About Us: Readings from Readings 3*, ed. Sharon Bakar (Kuala Lumpur, 2016).

"Kadaram" first appeared in *Cha:An Asian Literary Journal* 23, 2014.

One day, when everyone in the house had gone out somewhere, she wandered away from home in sheer misery and found herself walking outside town. There she saw a deserted old house. It was in ruins and had no roof. She went in and suddenly felt lonelier and more miserable than ever; she found she couldn't bear to keep her miseries to herself any longer. She had to tell someone.

- "Tell It To The Walls", Tamil folktale,
translated by A.K. Ramanujan

Jungle Without Water

The refidex seemed almost as big as the Holy Granth
Sahib. Jogi imagined his mother's surprise at the notion
of a book that only existed to tell how to travel around a
city. Jogi tucked his water bottle under his arm and rifled
through the pages, not sure of the names, numbers,
grids, or alphabets. He'd learnt English in Jallandhar, by
cramming under the fluorescent lights of the Gurdwara
office. Yet the names here in Brisbane continued to
surprise. For every Stafford and Hamilton, there were
places named Toowong, Taringa, and even Nundah. It
sounded like his friend Nanda's name. On his first night
in the city, Jogi had foolishly suggested to his friends
that they should visit The Gabba, the great cricket
stadium. They had flailed around, looking for signs. It
had taken them three weeks to understand it was spelled
Woolloongabba everywhere. The anti-climactic comp-
lexity of the name had been disappointing.

Jogi peered closely at the refidex, ignoring the heat
and his thirst. Australian college recruiters had told him
English names were simple. Johns and Simons and Eds
and Henrys. Jogi was glad for his own, short for
Joginder. His friends Satvinder, Bhupinder and Kailash
had no such luck. They smiled and laughed along with
the customs officers and phone company operators who

mangled their names.

The lady in black across the counter tried to tell Jogi how to use the book. "You look at the street first, here," she said, rifling through the first few pages with her red nails. "And then you look up the page it said, and the location of the street according to the letters and numbers on the grid alongside the relevant page. Okay?" Jogi nodded. She spoke very loudly, even though it was a library and she worked there.

Jogi's mind was still foggy. His mother had called at two o'clock that morning from Jallandhar, sobbing. "They have finally done it, my *puttar*," she said. "The transfer letter is here. Your father refuses to open it." Originally in the Army, Jogi's father now worked behind a desk at the Registrar's office, after Jogi's grandmother had feigned a heart attack and asked him to come back from the Kashmir border. The security of a job in bureaucracy stifled him, made him ask questions of his superiors, made him conspicuous, unpopular. He knew it too.

"You should go, *puttar*," he had said, when Jogi had showed his application papers to study in Australia. "There is no point in doing anything here. In the white man's country you can do anything you want, be anyone you want. Nobody will say anything. I am with you." On the day Jogi left, he carried a passport and visa and enrolment documents worth his family's savings. Around fifty relatives came to see him off, full of tears, fears and free advice.

At the library, Jogi realised he still had no answer. He asked again. "Please, ma'am," he said. "Please, I want to know where Gurdwara."

"Yes, and as I said, I don't know what that is, but – "

"Temple, temple, ma'am."

"Yes, well, that may be the case, but I'm afraid I still don't know where it is. And that's why this," she said, pointing to the refidex, "can help you. If you know the street where this temple is – "

"No, no street, ma'am."

This time the woman didn't hide her sigh. "I can only do so much, I'm afraid, I – "

"Okay, okay ma'am." Jogi was used to the frustrations of people over counters. He had heard his father's complaints. His father did not like having to follow all procedures to the letter. He did not like the rich ones who came to his desk, ready with bribes. He especially did not like their complaints to those above when he refused them. Even when warned that he'd be transferred to a jungle without water, remote and pointless.

"It is in two weeks, *beta*!" Jogi's mother wailed on the phone. "To Qadian of all places. What are we to do?"

"It will be okay, Ma," he said, not believing himself. "Is there any way out?"

"What way is there? Your cousin Jasvinder has said he knows some people, will go talk to them. But your father said nothing. He must do something too, na!"

Jogi had no words.

"Jogi, will you do something for me?"

"Anything, Ma."

"Will you do the Japji Sahib prayer with a Baba for your father? Your prayers always work. Since you were little."

Jogi went through the refidex again. Lists, maps, Brisbane, Gold Coast. None of it made sense. It was new to think finding a place to pray would be this hard.

*

In a family that liked staying put, Jogi had been the wayward child. "Like his father," his mother would say, when he was a boy. Couldn't keep still. Always getting into scrapes.

At the age of ten, he was sent home from school for beating up two other boys. At fourteen his limbs were full of bruises, and there was a black eye every few months. He lied that they were from cricket matches. His father's thrashings when he brought home his report card didn't help.

But his arrest at eighteen was different. A girl had filed a report of harassment. Jogi said it was love. He was being true to his feelings, and only wanted to express them, to communicate with her. He had waited outside her home, her school, her tuition class, her basketball stadium. He had never understood why she filed the complaint.

His uncle paid the bail as his father refused to step into the police station. A bad name on the family, he had said.

"If you don't want to be my father, I don't want to be your son," Jogi said when he reached home. That night was the worst beating in his memory.

After that, Jogi's mother conscripted him. He was to follow her to the Gurdwara, the neighbourhood temple, every Sunday. He hated the place. "So boring, we do nothing but sit," he said. "Listen to what they're saying," said his mother. Jogi did. At first it made no sense. He wished he was in the kitchens instead, volunteering to cook the temple fare, and chatting to other men. But nobody wanted him to touch the sacred *langar*, not after his arrest. So he sat with his mother, a mountain of boredom, and listened to the prayers. He listened. And listened. He realised they were repetitive. He began to recognise words. He heard the same words from his mother and sisters when they prayed at home. He began following them on his tongue. They brought a strange comfort.

He then began reading the parts he knew in the Guru Granth Sahib at home. Sometimes the verses made no sense, and it bothered him, but he kept going with the knowledge that what had been strange boring noises made sense today, and with the faith that they would make more sense tomorrow.

In this way, Jogi fell out of the habit of fighting, and in love with reading. He began liking his studies, and he began to do well in school. In time, his marks improved, and he brought his report card home casually. He was no longer afraid.

At the same time, something else emerged, and his mother was the first to notice. When mango season arrived, Jogi mentioned a craving for alphonsos. His mother said she had no time to go to the market, and joked that he should pray with the Guru Granth Sahib, and recite the Japji Sahib for his mangoes. Jogi laughed, and later when his mother spotted him at the house shrine, eyes closed, lips moving, she smiled to herself. Two weeks later, a gunny sack full of alphonso mangoes arrived at the doorstep, a gift from her husband's friend. She thought nothing of it.

Then, another time, Jogi told his mother about the girl he had been following, that he still thought of her. Not knowing what to say, Jogi's mother had simply told him to pray. When the girl showed up at Jogi's house sometime later, Jogi was as surprised as the rest of them – it had not been his doing, he insisted. The girl said she was there to invite the family to her cousin's wedding, but something about Jogi's surprise unnerved his mother, and she began watching him more closely whenever he recited the Japji Sahib in front of the Guru Granth Sahib. She had heard of such things in her family, though she had never been witness to it. A strange gene of sincerity embedded through the generations.

Still, she kept silent about it, until the rains that destroyed her brother's fields. Jogi prayed. When her brother reported the unnatural sliver of sun as a saving grace, Jogi's mother merely nodded to herself in confirmation.

Outside the State Library, Jogi thrust his photocopied sheaf of maps into Sandeep's hands. They walked across the bridge into the city. Sandeep perused and discarded half the pages. Jogi arched up at the sky and finished his water from the bottle. The sky burnt blue, the only thing that felt the same as Jallandhar. Everything else, even this new habit of carrying bottled water around, was a scene from a film. They looked around for a rubbish bin when they reached the Queen Street Mall.

"People put away their rubbish here," Sandeep had said, when Jogi had remarked on how clean everything in Brisbane was. "Not like back home. If you get caught littering here, you pay a fine." Since then Jogi always checked if there was a bin nearby before buying anything.

"Jogi, that is a perfectly good bottle," said Sandeep now, adjusting his glasses. "We can use it to take water from home when we go out."

"Why? Don't they have taps in the streets here?" Jogi asked. Sandeep sighed. It was his I-have-been-here-longer-than-you sigh.

Sandeep had arrived in Brisbane a full three weeks

before Jogi, and never let Jogi forget that. Sitting next to Jogi in English class, Sandeep leaned over Jogi's paper one day and finished his grammar test for him. They had stuck together ever since.

"They have water coolers here, but you must remember they have a water crisis," Sandeep said.

Jogi had heard much about this water crisis, but he didn't understand it. There were no water trucks bringing tanks of water to the suburbs. There were no protests, no rationing. Rather, from every tap Jogi and his friends touched in their tiny apartment, water gushed forth in full force, every hour of every day. Jogi honestly could not see the crisis.

They took a train to Burbank the next day, going by the list Sandeep found in the refidex. "A Hindu *mandir*," he said, and before Jogi could respond, continued, "I know, Jogi, you're Sikh and need a Gurdwara. But think, it's very far from here, more than three train zones away. Costs so much money. What is wrong with a *mandir*? You've been to many in India, na?" They sat by the train window. Jogi looked out of the window a lot, trying to read the big English signs.

"Yes, Sandeep, but only if there is no Gurdwara available. Here, if we know there is one, why – "

"I'm trying to save you money, *yaar*. People find ways to cut costs here, not like back home. Anyway they say all gods were one. A prayer to any one of them has the same effect." And he laughed, pleased with his logic.

Jogi tuned him out. The signs, he noticed, sometimes had in-built jokes in them. He tried to understand what they were.

It was three in the afternoon when they arrived in Burbank, and the suburb was in a sleepy heat. The *mandir*, to quote Sandeep, was not like home either. Jogi felt it when he knelt to prostrate himself, when he looked up at the marble deities in a makeshift altar that looked new and temporary. Sandeep lingered behind, letting Jogi go ahead. His bare feet felt cool on the cement floor, but otherwise there was nothing. Jogi looked at the priest Sandeep had brought in specifically for the occasion. Jogi imagined Sandeep had accomplished it by banging on his door, impervious to his pleas of "Morning prayers over, evening prayers at 6pm". Jogi wiped the back of his neck with a handkerchief, anticipating sweat despite the dry heat.

The man was now smiling at Jogi, sitting cross-legged by the altar. It was a wide smile that didn't go beyond his stretched lips. Jogi saw no teeth. It was a smile reserved for the stupidly faithful, handing over coins and notes in exchange for mantras.

Sandeep sat on the floor by the entrance, and though Jogi knew it was out of respect for the proceedings, he wished he were closer.

The priest opened his mouth to say something. Jogi stood up, knowing the priest's intent, not wanting to participate.

"My son, twenty dollars for a personal blessing." The priest's words sounded reflexive. They had been said a million times. Sandeep was already looking for his wallet.

"Let's go, *yaar*." Jogi said, turning around.

"Twenty dollars is okay, I will pay for now, and – "

"It's not the money."

"Then?"

"I cannot pray here."

"Why?"

But Jogi was already outside, feeling the stinging sun.

14

*

Two days later, Jogi was laughing in front of bald white men with sandalwood markings. They were silent but looked puzzled. Sandeep stood behind Jogi, and Jogi could sense him cringing.

The first time Jogi saw their kind, he had been in Australia a whole week. After Friday classes, he had huddled with Bhupinder and Satvinder around the big Hungry Jack's in the city, and when they heard cymbals and drums, they thought they were so homesick they were conjuring home sounds.

It was the first thing Jogi asked Sandeep about, when Sandeep brought up them and their temple in Graceville.

"They are ISKCON people," he said, pronouncing it "IS-KAAHN". "White Hindus. They sing 'Hare Krishna' a lot."

On the day they visited, they were told there were special prayers being held to end the water crisis. Jogi was surprised the temple structure was a wooden bungalow, a standard Queenslander among the many in the street. It was as if they were visiting a friend, despite the arriving crowds, and the informality of it seemed odd. Jogi took off his shoes at the entrance, staring at the innumerable white Australians clad in cotton saris and dhotis, some of them sporting various marks on their foreheads. It was a task to get inside the room where the prayers were conducted before the deities. The deity images, Jogi noticed, were Bengali in design. They looked jarringly authentic.

"Hare Krishna, my brother," said a tall, reedy-looking man next to Jogi, eyes glazed. Jogi did not respond.

A man at the front of the crowd, who seemed some sort of head priest, asked everyone to sit down. He wore saffron robes, was bald except for a tuft of hair at the back, and had sandalwood markings on his forehead. He looked like any holy man from India, except for his skin. Champions at handling crowds, Sandeep and Jogi quickly found a spot by a wall, where they could rest their backs. The head priest started talking about Krishna, and a man called Prabhupada, and quoted Hindu scriptures in numbers of chapters and verses, as if they had all been compiled and organised for the first time. The man was portly, with sallow skin and round, hard eyes. He spoke with a conviction that was at once alluring and fearful.

Twenty minutes in, Jogi fidgeted. "When am I going to do any prayers here, *yaar*?" he asked Sandeep.

"Patience, my friend. I spoke to them earlier. After this lecture, they call people out, for blessings. At that time, any prayers you want to do, just do it in front of them. I have already given them your name, they will call you."

"Really?"

"Yes, *yaar*. It is so much easier now, na, having organised everything before. See, planning works. This is how they do it here, all very effective. Not like back home."

Jogi sighed, and looked around. Some of the people around them were not really listening, either. Instead, there were drinks being passed around. Jogi and Sandeep knew by now that they were always thirsty in this new land, and did not say no when the drinks were offered to them. Within a few gulps they realised it was *bhang* – milk mildly laced with cannabis. Jogi wondered why the Hare Krishna people would serve *bhang*. It didn't seem very Krishna-esque. He turned to ask Sandeep, but his friend had a silly smile on, and Jogi realised it was too late. Either the *bhang* was very strong, or Sandeep was a far worse lightweight than he let on.

"Joginder Singh."

Jogi responded to the name, and stood up. Without knowing why, he quickly checked if he felt steady. He thought he was. The head priest, who'd called his name, now waited in silence as he made his way through the seated crowd to the front. He was aware Sandeep was following from behind.

The portly priest sat cross-legged on the floor, facing Jogi, his back to the deities. Jogi followed his example, and they were eye-to-eye. Jogi noticed other similarly clad men by the priest, all in saffron, all bald, except for the tuft at the back, all with sandalwood on their foreheads. They all looked the same. Jogi blinked. No, that could not be true. He looked again, more closely, scrutinising the faces. He was certain, and yet it was impossible. All the same, a similar shade of pink in the heat.

Jogi brought his palms together. "Please, I want to do the Japji Sahib," he said. Even as he heard the words, he felt it coming from someone else.

The men looked at him, then at each other, then back at him.

Jogi repeated his sentence.

They smiled. To Jogi even the smiles were the same – beatific and uncomprehending.

"My brother," said the head priest. "There is no greater prayer than Hare Krishna."

Jogi blinked. "Yes, maybe," he said, trying to be diplomatic. Surely they were joking. Who didn't know the Japji Sahib? How could a group of *bhang*-serving white Hindus not know it? They were playing with him. "But see, I have been asked to do this one."

"We don't do other prayers," said a thinner one to the

left of the head priest, cutting Jogi off. "Krishna is all. He is the First Creator, the One from whom everything emanates. The rest all come after Him, but He is the Godhead." His green eyes danced with enthusiasm, as if he believed he was making a profound statement. He proceeded to quote numbers and verses like the head priest had before, again as if they were the only ones of their kind. It reminded Jogi of the video jockeys he used to watch on MTV India, trying to familiarise himself with the language. "At the number one spot today, none other than Madonna, the great diva, who knows trends before they happen, who has the finger on the right pulse, always. There are many who try to fake their way through this, but really, we know who the original is, don't we, my darlings?"

Jogi tried hard not to smile. He could hear Sandeep shuffling his feet behind him, having opted not to sit down.

"Look," interrupted the head priest – perhaps he had noticed the smile – "It's just – we do not do other prayers. You are welcome to recite what you want, though. Krishna accepts everything."

The men around him looked at each other.

"But, the great founder Prabhupada said – " one of them started saying.

"Krishna accepts everything, my brother."

The man frowned but remained silent. They all then looked at Jogi, and he understood he was expected to begin, in their presence.

Jogi closed his eyes and tried to concentrate.

"*Ik Onkar, Satnam*," he said. The words rang out, touched the walls, the people around, the deities and the men sitting before them, and came back to Jogi. He felt nothing.

18

"*Karta purukh.*" Jogi opened his eyes a fraction. He could hear Sandeep's hard breathing, as if it were a task for him to stand still. The two men in the front continued smiling, trying to emulate the bliss of the deities behind them. Their skin was almost mottled in appearance. The sandalwood on their foreheads melted, slowly running down their nose. Jogi heard a fly buzzing. He heard his voice, croaking the powerful prayer, that made things happen. Somehow it was suddenly hilarious.

"*Nir paunh,*" he continued, trying to be serious.

"*Nir vaer,*" he could not help myself, and a giggle escaped. The two men blinked, puzzled.

"*Akaal moo* – " Jogi gave up, and collapsed into laughter. The sight of the offended-looking men only made him laugh harder.

"Jogi! What on earth are you doing?" He could hear Sandeep behind him, but could not pay attention. He barely even registered the rest of the crowd. He heared Sandeep apologising to the men as he was dragged away.

"Do you promise?"

"Arre, I promise, *yaar*. Really. No laughing this time."

Jogi and Sandeep entered the Gurdwara at Kuraby. It had been nearly a two-hour trip. It was three days after the Hare Krishna excursion, almost a week since Jogi's mother's call. Sandeep and Jogi had been very hungry and sleepy after visiting Graceville, a result of the *bhang*. Since then, the requirement of a Gurdwara had become more pressing. Jogi's mother's had called again, expressing surprise that the prayers had yet to be performed. Sandeep found out about a public holiday when their teacher explained the long weekend, gave extra homework, and wished the class Happy Easter as she left.

This time they travelled with two water bottles. The mid-afternoon heat was enough to wilt their wits. Jogi noticed Sandeep periodically emerging with water in the bottles, but knew better than to ask where it had come from. He would only say it was from a clean source, that there was no water contamination here, not like back home.

Jogi began to comprehend a certain lack in the Brisbane air. It didn't have the heavy caress of humidity. The sun pricked his skin directly, like little needles. And there was a burning sensation that did not go away, even after a shower. There was also an atmosphere of thirst about the place. The wind was dry, and Jogi's bookshelves had a perennial film of grey particles despite daily dusting. Foliage on the street was only occasionally green, and mud-caked cars churned up more dirt as they sped by. There was a tinderbox feel to the city. For the first time Jogi wondered how Australians endured this on a yearly basis.

When Jogi took off his shoes at the Gurdwara entrance, he noticed a bucket of water and a cup next to an outdoor tap. He washed his feet judiciously, careful to scoop water into his hands to wet his heels. He adjusted his turban before stepping inside. Sandeep tied a handkerchief as a bandana to cover his head.

It was cool and dark within, with the altar holding the Guru Granth Sahib at the far end. The very sight of it was reassuring. Jogi sighed, and Sandeep muttered in approval. Jogi took a swig of water, going towards a benign Baba smiling from the altar.

"All yours. No need to thank me. Just make sure you don't laugh," said Sandeep, and Jogi wanted to hug him.

The Baba seemed already to know what was needed.

Thanks to Sandeep's organising, Jogi suspected. After their customary bow to the Guru Granth Sahib, Jogi and the Baba sat cross-legged on the floor by the altar, facing each other. The Baba, with his long greying beard and rosaries, was straight out of Jogi's weekly dreams of home. His Punjabi was flawless, his eyes kind, his voice compassionate. Jogi wanted to tell him all about his father, the job, the transfer, his mother's fear, his confusion. He wanted the man to listen to him, to reassure him in Punjabi, to show him the Japji Sahib prayer in Gurmukhi so that he may read from his native script, though he knew the prayer by heart. Sandeep sat cross-legged at the back, all ears.

"Your name, my son?" asked the Baba, and for some reason Jogi did not like his choice of address.

"Joginder," he said after a pause, much softer than he expected.

"Your full name, my son."

Jogi tried not to wince, and found it difficult to respond. Sandeep noticed and provided the answer. "Joginder Singh Dhariwal, Baba."

"We are praying for your father today?" the Baba asked Jogi. Jogi's eyes were on the Baba's right fingers, twirling his rosary. It was held together by tough red string, knotted after 108 beads.

"Yes, we are," said Sandeep, and nudged Jogi from behind.

Jogi searched inside himself, with a sinking feeling. He pushed it aside and tried to summon the more familiar sense of emptying his mind, making space in a mental ether for the words to come forth. He found none. It wasn't the places after all. Not that the external conditions had to be just right. He could not conjure words at the command of other people – not even his mother, nor for his father. Praying out of obligation was just stupid.

"We can do the Japji Sahib three times, or if you want, more than that, in multiples of three," said the Baba, now scrutinising Jogi more closely. Jogi noticed that the red knot of his rosary had frayed edges, indicating their age. He still had no words.

"Jogi!" whispered Sandeep, but Jogi did not turn around. Sandeep said to the Baba, "The poor boy, he is missing home a lot, he has suddenly become so shy, he struggles a lot with his English, maybe now he has forgotten his Punjabi." He laughed aloud. Neither Jogi nor the Baba joined in, and Sandeep's laughter echoed off the walls and ceiling before petering out.

"Never mind, my son," said the Baba, addressing Jogi again. "Let's recite the prayer." He placed a prayer book between them, written in Gurmukhi. The script was soothing, reminding Jogi of early mornings at the Amritsar Golden Temple, where all the signs leading to the water tank were in the same script. They had followed the signs as children, immersing their feet in the tank for a rush of cold that brought down their entire body temperatures before entering sacred grounds.

"Lets start," said the Baba. "*Ik Onkar, Satnam.*"

Jogi closed my eyes, dipped his head down. Nothing.

"*Karta purukh. Nir paunh, nir vaer.*"

Still nothing. His lips were mute, he could not utter a sound. He opened his mouth but sensed the barrier. He buried his face in his hands, noiseless in his frustration. There was no way he could explain this to Sandeep.

He heard Sandeep's deep sigh behind him.

"Sandeep, listen to me, yaar, it's not like I planned it, na." Jogi said, as they walked down Elizabeth Street. Jogi barely registered the afternoon sun hitting his eyes, almost blinding his sight of the footpath.

"Jogi, enough, I don't see any further point in this."

Jogi and Sandeep had got off the train at Milton when Jogi's apologies had failed to placate his three-week senior, and he did not know where they were heading now.

"Please, Sandeep, you have to help me find a – "

"Help? Isn't that what I've been doing this entire past week?"

Jogi stopped walking, sheepish. Sandeep continued ahead. He did not look back. Traffic whizzed by, oblivious to the fighting Indians on the footpath.

"Sandeep, you must let me explain," he said, trying not to cough in the arid traffic dust. Sandeep froze, turned around and walked back towards his friend. He took Jogi's empty water bottle from his hand. "Okay, yes, tell me. Now. Tell me. What's to explain? You walk out of the Hindu *mandir*, laugh at the IS-KAAHN people, and play dumb with your own Baba priest. What is your problem, huh? Does His Royal Highness need to have the entire Amritsar brought to him before he says the dear prayers his mummy wants him to?" Sandeep walked away again, and Jogi rushed after him, trying to catch up. Sandeep went to a water cooler to fill up their bottles, but the faucet seemed faulty and no water poured out. In frustration Sandeep kicked the cooler. Water trickled out of the faucet, drip-drip-dripping into the basin. Sandeep's efforts with the tap did nothing. He kicked it again.

"You know what, I deserve this," he said to the faucet, knowing Jogi was within earshot. "Instead of studying, or working, or even going to the movies, I had to run around Brisbane looking at your bloody refidex, find you a place to pray. Because mamma's boy can't even do that himself. This is the problem with you people." Sandeep turned around and faced his friend. "Always expecting others to do things for you. Not wanting to be independent, to solve your problems on your own." He paused. "Why did that librarian give you the refidex, Jogi, and not just tell you what you want to know? Because she is not your servant. You were expected to find things out yourself. Be independent." Jogi knew what was coming next. "That is what it's like here. Not like in India, always depending on – "

"Shut up!" said Jogi, grabbing Sandeep's collar. Sandeep froze, and his eyes widened. Jogi noticed it and let go of him, straightening himself.

"You always say this place is better than India. For everything!" said Jogi. "Maybe you have forgotten things easily, but I have not. You may know so much, but you don't know what its like to be so far away, in a place where everything works, but you don't know how to make it work, so you're always left out. Out of everything. People here have their parents here, their brothers, sisters, cousins here. They have their loves here, their lives here. They help each other. Who am I going to go to for help if not you? When I know things better here who am I going to help if not someone like you?"

Sandeep said nothing but stood as he was, staring. Jogi felt they had been paused in a film scene, and to break the feeling he looked away, across the street.

"So you think this is all easy for me?" asked Sandeep, his voice low. "Yes, Mr Jogi, I'm just walking around all day, with temple directions coming out of my ears. And I do it because it's so much damn fun." Jogi registered Sandeep's sarcasm. "Jogi, I'm going home."

"Sandeep, look – "

"No, *yaar*. Don't follow me. I have to go. I'll talk to you later."

Jogi watched Sandeep walk away. He would have to talk to him tomorrow, tell him about how he could not pray for his father even as he really wanted to. He began walking, looking for familiar signs that would lead him back to his rental place.

Jogi saw the church when he turned a corner. The doors were open, and several people were entering, walking from parked cars around the area. He strode closer to the church, and noticed that the inside was semi-dark, barely lit.

He sat on a bench by the church compound, too nervous to enter. It would be highly unusual for a turbaned brown man to attend the Easter church service. Instead, he watched the families still outside, greeting others, making their way in.

A girl in a yellow dress, standing by her mother, smiled at him. He smiled back. She must be around twelve or thirteen, thought Jogi.

She walked up to him, while her parents were in deep conversation with another family. She stopped a few paces away, and smiled again.

"Hello," she said.

"Hello," said Jogi.

"I'm Alice".

"I'm Jogi."

Alice nodded, weighing the name. The ribbon around her pigtail waved in the breeze.

"Where are you from?"

"India."

"Oh." It was clear Alice had no idea what India was.

"Where are you from?" asked Jogi.

"What?"

"I said, where are you from?" Jogi expected her to laugh, find the question silly, or just say "Brisbane". Instead, Alice thought hard.

"I'm from my mother."

Jogi found the answer unexpectedly touching. He extended his hand. Alice stepped forward and took it, and they solemnly shook on it.

Alice's eyes were the same kind of blue as the Brisbane sky, thought Jogi. Bright, clear, and occasionally too innocent to understand anything else but that blue was possible.

"Do Indians celebrate Easter?" asked Alice. Jogi thought about it.

"Some of them, yes," he said. Alice took this as proof of something. She nodded in sage agreement. "My mum says all kinds of people do Easter. Even if we don't see them, doesn't mean that they don't, like, the Indians who do Easter would do the Easter egg-hunt, right?"

Jogi was lost, barely trying to keep up. "Eggs?"

"Yeah. Easter eggs. In the morning."

"What happens to the eggs?"

"No, no, like..." Alice struggled to explain. She sat next to Jogi on the bench. "Like, the Easter bunny comes with the Easter eggs, and hides it in your garden, all these different colourful ones, and you hunt for it when you wake up, and you get to keep the ones you find."

"Oh."

"Yeah, except that, well, I think there's no Easter bunny and my parents do the hiding, but that's okay. I like pretending like I'm finding the eggs the Bunny has left behind."

Jogi smiled. "You like to pretend?"

Alice smiled back. "Yeah! It's fun. It's my own secret."

She became thoughtful again. "My history teacher Mrs Yeong says everyone has pretended at some point. She said a long time ago, like, my parents' grandparents' grandparents and more were sent here from England, like prisoners, and they were sent here because it was away from everywhere else, like a jungle without water, and like it was so impossible to be here, that being here was the punishment, the prison. But everyone pretended it was okay, and so it was okay, people survived."

The humidity was so bad people fanned themselves with paper as they walked into the church. Alice took a breath, as Jogi digested her words.

"Everyone's going in," said Alice. "We should go in too." She stood up, then turned around. "Coming?"

"Alice!" Jogi heard a woman calling.

"That's my mum. I should go. Come on!"

Alice turned around and ran to her mother as Jogi stood up, but he didn't follow her. Sweat ran in rivulets down his face and back, and his head ached. He swallowed hard. The knot in his throat had nothing to do with the humidity.

As the hymns inside the church began, Jogi dipped his head and clasped his hands. He closed his eyes. The Japji Sahib came to his lips. It flowed easily through him, without barrier. He bowed his head further, and heard thunder in the distance. He inhaled, and without realising, thought of water. From the mineral water bottle, from taps, from buckets, from fountains, from wells, from rivers, from the ocean. The sweat made his shirt stick to his back. He felt a cool breeze. He caught his breath for two seconds, and all was utterly silent. He then let go.

The service inside the church continued. Jogi sensed a wetness streaming down his cheeks that was not sweat.

Another roll of thunder. he began walking home. He was no longer thirsty.

On the way it began pouring with rain.

The Lovely Village

A lovely village on the far side once decided to erect a fence up around itself. It was a tall, white fence, always glistening in the sun as if it had just been painted. It provided a very great protection to the village, standing so resolutely and completely around its space, at the border of the village. It let out some of the people of the village when they needed to visit far off places, but it was only for them that it would open.

The village was a charming village full of honest, industrious people who loved work and loved play, and had an earnest mayor who took his position of serving the village very seriously. They worked on land that was endlessly fertile, responding to very predictable seasons that ensured rain and sun at just the right times. The winters were not too miserable and the summers were glorious. There were not too few of them as to feel they were left out of the progress evident in other villages, nor were they too many for there to be a surfeit of people as opposed to opportunity.

Over years, some in the village also fought hard for everybody else's right to equality, which resulted in a sameness between the rich and the poor, the women and the men, the animals and the humans. It eventually became clear that everyone in this village lived a highly worthy life indeed, and the villagers were very proud of this truth. The Lord Mayor informed everyone they were right to be proud, and to keep it uppermost in their minds as they did the work they loved, as carpenter, or butcher, or gatekeeper, or painter.

As the fame of the village spread, some newcomers turned up at the fence. One day, one of the newcomers decided to talk to the gatekeeper. "Dear gatekeeper," he said, "your village is so lovely, will you not let us in?"

"Oh, how I wish I could, how dearly, but honestly, I cannot," said the gatekeeper.

"But why," responded the newcomer, "why will you not let us into this truly enchanted place, this place that you must so clearly love?"

"Oh yes, how I do love this place, but see, I am not authorised to let you in, even if I wanted to, I would lose my job if I did, and in this village nobody lets go of their work."

The newcomer agreed this was a high virtue indeed. But he and more of his kind were still on the other side of the fence, so he called out to those who were passing by, "Sir, ma'am, how lovely you are, will you please give the gatekeeper permission to let me and my friends in?"

At first nobody seemed to hear, but then a little girl looked for the voice and shrieked when she found the source. "Oh, Mummy, oh look how ugly it is!" Upon which the little girl's mother bent down to shush her gently, and explained why it was never nice or polite to say bad things about other people, and that the little should show some character and apologise to the different-looking man.

The newcomer encouraged his friends to speak also, and continued asking to be let in. They agreed and joined in asking those who were close to the fence to help them, and this upset the gatekeeper.

"Why do you keep troubling the good, innocent folk of this village? They have done nothing to you," he said.

"We only ask to be let in, good sir, perhaps if enough people hear us, one of them will," said the newcomer.

Over the next few days, more and more people of the village heard the requests as they were going on with their fruitful day. They talked among themselves about the newcomers, and in the end decided it would be best to have a meeting with the Lord Mayor.

The meeting took place at the centre of the village, and everyone was invited, even the gatekeepers. The Lord Mayor stood on a raised platform and looked down on everyone else gathered around him. Once he was sure everyone was present, he started, "I will now call this council to order. We are here today, at this eighty-seventh gathering, considering the issue of some of our members who have happened to be near the fence, being harassed and deprived of their peaceful enjoyment of the day. It is the objective of this meeting to find a fair and peacable solution to this, with of course equal input from all parties."

Mr Priest, who had once been Lord Mayor and wasn't anymore but was planning to be one again, said "And you make sure that input is really equal, Justin, as I'm right here witnessing everything, unlike the last issue, I seem to remember, when I had been away."

"Nothing unequal was done the last time, Tom, just as it will not be right now, despite what you may think, so you may rest assured," said the Lord Mayor.

Martha cleared her throat, "The newcomers have been requesting my daughter to assist the gatekeeper in accessing the door of the fence to permit entry," she said in one breath, then gulped for air, glad to have spoken up.

"You know I will never do such a thing, sir, not without direct orders from you," said the gatekeeper immediately. "It's why I'm eager for today's decision, perhaps more so than anyone else."

"Why are the newcomers here?" asked Geoff, an honest man who loved working with wood in his carpentry and was genuinely curious. Phil the dentist rolled his eyes before answering "Well, why would they not be here? Look around you, my man. Our trees and plants yield twice a year, our cows give milk endlessly, our houses are sturdy, we have a good mayor (Mr Priest grumbled at this), nobody steals or murders, and we all do what we want to do, everything is as it should be. Of course they want to come here."

"So can we permit access then?" asked Natalie, who was ten years old and had seen the newcomers talking to her parents through a gap between the planks. The Lord Mayor turned to lawyer Albert, who came forward with the legal books in his hand. "I'm terribly afraid there is a problem. There is nothing in here about newcomers or permission or access."

"Oh but surely there must be something there that accepted the past newcomers!" said Anastasia. The Lord Mayor nodded, and the others whispered among themselves. Why, yes, they did remember other newcomers in the past having been allocated. They had looked, talked, and cooked like them. Nobody could point them out today. Some of them had had children who'd only ever known the village.

"That was rather a long time ago, ladies and gentlemen," explained lawyer Albert with great patience. "It was a different time, it is an altogether separate issue that confronts us today."

"In all fairness, Albert, I do need to consider, does anyone possess any divergent views on this?" asked the Lord Mayor.

"I am shocked and appalled at all of you," said a booming voice, and everyone knew who it belonged to – the respected Tara, who strode majestically up to the raised platform with the rest of her supporters. Tara enjoyed a very special position in the village. She was one of the very few who did not have to work for a living, as she claimed her real purpose was to observe and comment on things that happened in the village. Her contributions in the past had been significant, and the crowd parted to let her majestic bearing through.

"There is nothing wrong with their request," she pronounced heavily, so as to make even the Lord Mayor quake a little. "We have acquiesced to such requests before, and we can do so again," And she stood with such great conviction that it must have been infectious, for some of the villagers around her nodded to themselves as well.

"Now, now, just you wait there," said Mr Priest, and Tara's companions groaned aloud. "Just because you say this, doesn't mean it can be done. Sure, we as the lovely village, proud of our equality, want to do the right thing, but just as we have faith that we have such a fine workable system in Albert's lawbooks, so must we also abide by it to guide us to the right decision."

There were some murmurs of approval at this, even a "hear, hear," and even the Lord Mayor was moved enough to dip his head a couple of times in agreement.

"It is a faulty system!" cried Tara, and her minions took the call up, repeating it several times to those around them. Instead of the electrifying effect Tara had depended on to keep Tara as Tara all this time, the rest

33

just seemed disgruntled.

"Don't fault the system," said Nathan.

"It is a good system," said Charles.

"The system has never failed us," croaked old Paul.

"The system is responsible for what we are," said Margaret, who received a chorus of approval.

"The system *is* responsible for us," said Tara, changing tracks instantly. "It should also provide for the newcomers then."

"I'm absolutely assured it does," said lawyer Albert, as if given a personal challenge. "The system functions for the protection of the village at all costs."

"Exactly, Albert," the Lord Mayor interjected, "the village needs to be protected. It has been protected all this while, which is how we constructed everything and everyone equal, and we are so proud of it, and that's the truth."

"Hear, hear."

"Well said, Lord Mayor."

Tara cleared her throat, not so majestic anymore. "All I'm saying," she said slowly, "is to include newcomers in the system."

"Well, yes," said young Sue, with some exasperation, "but how many are we talking?"

"Only the most deserving ones," said David.

"Only those who understand our system," said Louise.

"And follow the rules," said George.

"And don't do unequal things," said Desmond.

"Are there many of them?" asked Cheryl, and even the Lord Mayor blinked, not having thought of this.

"Too many, too many," said old Paul. "How will we hold them?"

"We will then no longer be us," said Aunt Bertha.

"We need self-protection," echoed Jay.

"We must follow the system for our protection," agreed Claire.

"I am afraid, Lord Mayor," said Agatha, stepping forward towards the dais, past Tara. "I am afraid what we truly need is proper protection for us to be us, and this is dire, and urgent, and we don't know if you can see that, sir."

"That's right," said Mr Priest. "This is unequivocal evidence of very poor leadership, and I applaud the people of this village for seeing that so quickl – "

"Now, now, Tom," said the Lord Mayor. "It has long been known that I work only to serve the village, that is by the system and the people know I follow the system. It is how we practice our equality, which makes this the place we are so proud of, and that is the truth. And if its protection that's necessary, then protection it is."

When the matter looked nearly settled, and the Lord Mayor could nearly give a sigh of relief, Charlotte said "However, I am doubtful, perplexed even, that we champion our protection when that fence is so rickety."

"Absolutely," said Mr Priest.

"What's wrong with the fence?" asked Tara, and only her companions could tell she was genuinely puzzled.

"Well, it says here," said lawyer Albert, with a quiet triumph, "that it is to protect the fragile perfection of this village."

"It can't do that the way it is right now," said old Paul. "There are way too many gaps and cracks, which show us the outside."

"And they show our inside the other way too," observed Mary with gravity, and there was much nodding.

"So it is established," said Mr Priest with authority,

interrupting Tara, who had begun to speak. "What we need to do immediately – "

" – is board up the fence, to make it stronger," finished the Lord Mayor, hurrying to get ahead of Mr Priest.

"Hear, hear."

"Keep our equality safe."

"Lets protect ourselves!"

Tara, try as she might, could not get a word in edgeways, even as she knew this meant her role would remain necessary for still a while.

And so the villagers worked together, in blissful harmony, in perfect symphony, to strengthen the fence that gave the village and its equality such beautiful protection. The carpenter had the wood and nails and tools, the painter had paint, and the welder brought especial delight when he offered some of his expensive metals, and he and the blacksmith inserted durable sheets of steel and aluminium. They even inserted strong metal nuts and bolts on the door the gatekeeper used to let the villagers in and out, so that the entry and exit would be smoother. Tara and her companions didn't help, but knew they didn't need to, because their role was still valid and required in the village. It was a great day of co-operation, sharing, and mutual understanding. They all then went home to celebrate in quiet joy. There had been a peacable outcome, everyone was still the same, everyone was equal and proud and happy, and that is the truth.

Green Grass

When Mohan's wife arrived in Thirumugam we could hardly believe it. Her skin was white, so white that we could not see where her hair started. Once we looked closely, we saw that her hair was golden, like our paddy on the eve of harvest day. The two of them climbed down from the Ambassador car in front of Ammani Mami's house, where they were to stay for a few weeks. We were slightly disappointed. Little Nandu had run around the village for days yelling that Mohan and his white wife from Australia were coming, that Mohan was now very rich, that they had a cellphone each, and drove shiny foreign cars. His news resounded in our cluster of mud huts. When we waited outside Ammani Mami's big brick house, though, all we saw was an Ambassador car pull up, with her nephew inside. The Ambassador was something we saw everyday – even our school headmaster sometimes used it to get to town.

Mohan's wife was introduced to us as Ray-chil. It was her first time in India. We saw them go into Ammani Mami's house. Ammani Mami was Mohan's father's third cousin, and single-handedly brought up Mohan after his parents died. We were very happy to see that Mohan remembered his relations here in Thirumugam, and that his wife Ray-chil was honourable enough to pay her respects to her husband's relations.

We heard a lot about Ray-chil in the next few days, and quite a bit about Mohan as well. It was all Nandu's doing. Nandu visited Ammani Mami's house a few times a week. Her son Velan taught Nandu 8th Standard Math. But when Mohan and Ray-chil came, Nandu found excuses to visit them everyday. We saw Ray-chil and Mohan around Thirumugam a lot, and when we didn't, Nandu would tell us all that we needed to know.

Mohan and Ray-chil had met and fallen in love in Australia while studying. Her divorced parents were not invited to the wedding. Having them together in the same room would remind Ray-chil of her childhood, smelling of citronella, scratching her body acne, wearing peasant blouses and standing pointlessly next to her mother at rallies. Nandu said he wasn't sure what all this meant, only that these were reasons for Ray-chil insisting on coming to Thirumugam for her honeymoon. Mohan did not have the option of saying no.

Ray-chil loved Thirumugam and we loved her right back. She came to our riverbanks in the mornings, where we washed our clothes and ourselves. She smiled at our stares, and in television English once said, "It's just so hot," to nobody in particular. "But I'm going to get some clothes stitched." Nandu repeated her words to us in Tamil, but we already understood her apologetic tone, about her jeans and bare arms. Mohan was with her, and when some of the men waved from the river and called out his name, he at first pretended he hadn't heard. They kept calling out to him, till Ray-chil turned towards him and said something too soft for us to hear. Mohan then turned around, and smiled and nodded at the men.

"Mohan is a foreigner now, he has no time for us," Chellamma said later that evening, as we walked back from the fields. "Yes, did you see, he hardly had any gifts for anyone," we responded. "Only his wife."

The next day we saw Ray-chil walking the streets, smiling at the small group of boys that had formed around her. The group eventually became so large Ray-chil and Mohan could no longer move. Mohan tried to shoo them away, but Ray-chil knelt down at their eye-level and spoke to them. She took their pictures and learnt some words. She seemed to already know some Tamil, and practised it on the boys, who would laugh, congratulate her, and teach her more words. Ray-chil was very clever, Pandi said. She knew how to make herself pleasing to Mohan's family. We guessed they must have married without his family's consent – but Mohan's family should have thought of these things before sending him to Chennai, and then Australia, to study. "Those that go so far away, lose a little bit of what they initially knew," said seventy-year-old Tenkasi. He would know, he's lost four sons to the big city. "They have to make space for new things, new ideas, new languages, new ways of thinking, and to fit it all in, some of the old things had to be pushed aside."

But Ray-chil seemed to know that, and seemed to be making up for it. One day she came to Manickam's sundry shop in the middle of the village, and asked him for a box of matches in just Tamil, without any English words. Manickam did not understand her accent at first, but he was very impressed, and, grinning, gave her the matches for free. Not long after, Nandu reported that she had been taking pictures of cows, and had turned up one morning at the milkman's house, asking if he would be so kind as to teach her how to milk one of his cows. That news spread very quickly, and some of us did not know what to make of it. We heard she had been alone –

39

Mohan wasn't with her. But she had genuinely just wanted to learn how to milk a cow. Besides, she was white – she would not have the same ideas of honour as us.

Still, Velan said he spoke to Mohan about it. And Velan was very diplomatic – he did not make it seem like a complaint. Had he told Ray-chil yet about Velan's grass, we asked? No, he was scared. He watched Ray-chil very carefully. Ray-chil and Mohan have never been up on the roof of Ammani Mami's house. We laughed.

Nandu's stories kept us entertained, but we were also a little concerned about Mohan. He was no longer the Mohan we remembered, the Mohan who would run to the river in nothing but red shorts and dust and splash in with a leap and a scream. He first arrived so stiff, so uncomfortable, as if he were the foreigner, not his new wife. He walked with her in his odd pants that had too many pockets and stopped at his knees, and shirts in thick material with collars. He looked like a Bombay film star, but still faded next to his smiling wife, from whose skin and hair the sunshine for our fields seemed to emanate. He almost always spoke English, even when Ray-chil tried to speak in Tamil.

But after Ray-chil's milkman episode, Mohan seemed to relax. Pandi thinks it happened after they all went to the cinema in the neighbouring town, Nandu in tow. They were showing an old movie, a Sivaji Ganesan mythology in whch the great actor played Lord Shiva. Apparently Mohan had burst out laughing at a small joke, and later explained it to Ray-chil. He had heard that joke before, he said, when he was in primary school. It was about punning on the word "hot". Dust from fruits collected on the ground had to be blown away, like blowing on hot food. Mohan laughed and laughed at this, and Ray-chil laughed a little with him, pretending to understand.

After that, we all agreed, Mohan seemed better. He would wear his old *veshti*, his white lower garments, speak in Tamil, and once Nandu spotted him using a neem twig to brush his teeth in the morning.

We don't think Mohan told Ray-chil anything about going to the milkman's house. Maybe he felt it was something beyond his wife's comprehension. But Ray-chil had become more and more like us as time wore on. She was now on laughing terms with Ammani Mami, and had started to learn her recipes – something we received dubiously from Nandu, as Ammani Mami was very particular about them. But Nandu insisted he saw it with his own eyes. He'd gone to Ammani Mami's house, since Ray-chil had called him. He had rushed from his homework like a shot. We didn't blame him – we noticed many of us, young and old, found excuses to go see Ray-chil, to touch her skin, feel her hair, hear her speak Tamil with such pink pink lips. But Ray-chil had not been there. She was out with Ammani Mami, who wanted to show her where she got some ingredients for her *avial* from.

"What did you do then?" we asked Nandu, a little jealous of Ray-chil for accessing Ammani Mami's secrets, and wanting to distract ourselves.

"Well, Mohan was there, and he gave me a gift," he said.

"Mohan gave you a gift? What was it?"

"A crystal pyramid."

"A what?"

"A crystal pyramid. He showed me how to use it. If you hold it at a certain angle to a light, the elements of light break into its individual components – the colours

41

of the rainbow. Mohan said I could use it in school later."

"You can see the rainbow in the pyramid?"

"No, you see it through the pyramid. The crystal is the prism. You see the bare elements through it. All the colours are there, but my favourite is green, because it is strong, and it reminds me of our fields."

But we had lost interest. Ray-chil was not in this story.

We all knew Velan was nervous having Ray-chil and Mohan around in the house. But we realised that over time, watching Ray-chil, Velan slowly changed his mind. He was as curious as us at first, at Ray-chil's eagerness. Initially Velan would answer her questions with his eyes on the floor, as if shielding them. He would laugh if she made a joke or made a mistake in her Tamil, but would then carry a guilty look about him. Gradually, though, Velan would look evenly into Ray-chil's eyes, and Nandu once reported that Velan himself had cracked a joke about the village well, and swelled when Ray-chil laughed. We understood completely. Not only did she look like the Americans on the television we'd crowd around in the schoolteacher's house, but she also ate our food and spoke our language – something that we never saw in that bright box.

We felt Velan must have changed his mind the day Ray-chil and Mohan visited the Kali Amman temple on the outskirts of Thirumugam. She was our village guardian, this Kali Amman. She made sure the rains came on time, and that we harvested enough each year. When Velan saw Ray-chil there, with her eyes closed and palms pressed together, he must have finally felt she was trustworthy.

She was dumbstruck, said Velan to us the next day. Overwhelmed. Velan had finally taken Ray-chil and

Mohan up to the roof, after they returned from the temple. "I show you view," he had said, using it as an excuse. But Ray-chil had seen it right away. They emerged from the side stairwell on the second floor of Ammani Mami's house onto the open-air cement rooftop. It was a large open space, perfect for summer nights when the house was simply too stifling. We knew the floor now had black stains, and the sides were crumbling, and the ground was littered with little seeds and flowers from the trees overhead. But in a corner, to the right of the house, Velan had set up something, something that showed foresight.

Ray-chil gasped when she saw it. Although she should have been struck by the greys, blues and reds of the thatched and cemented rooftops around her, what drew her eyes was a patch of the clearest, brightest green, right in front of her. It was in such contrast to the rest of the musty environment it almost seemed to glow. Ray-chil went closer.

"Why you son of a bitch, you waited this long to tell us?" Mohan said to Velan, who just glowed. He seemed to want to share his pride. "Emergency supplier," he said in English, drawing out each vowel, savouring the mouthful. His secret patches of grass came from the hands of gardeners and watchmen in landowner houses, and went to hotels and stadiums in towns and cities at a fraction of the market price. They were all the rage, he said. Everyone in the district came to him, just by word of mouth. "And also," he said, "it is re-cycling. Take one from old, give one to new. Take old grass, give new grass. No waste."

The patch of grass was rectangular, the size of three cricket pitches. It started from the rooftop door and seemed to lead to the far wall of the rooftop, from where one could look over the whole village and marvel at our squalor all in one go, not piecemeal over days. Mohan hedged away from the patch, turning slightly so that he stood at an angle from it, neither facing nor turning away from it. He said it hurt his eyes, and looked the other way into the mountains. Ray-chill seemed very drawn to it, however. She stood and stared at the secret stash, admiring the painstakingly nourished patch of first grade carpet grass. She even bent down to feel the blades with her fingers, caressing its velvety smoothness, running both her hands through them, feeling their over-cared for voluptuousness. She stayed that way until Mohan interrupted her. She then regained her bearings and attempted a small smile at her husband, a smile he did not return. Both of them told Velan he could trust them, they wouldn't tell anyone. Later, they found this was something they agreed on, that Velan was a genius.

All of us spoke about nothing but Ray-chil. She was in our thoughts when we started the day in the fields, and still there when we returned home. Manickam boasted as a complaint that he had run out of *Fair and Lovely* creams. He had ordered more, and when they arrived, sold them at a higher price, and still ran out. Ray-chil began to recognise some of us, especially the little girls, and remember our names. She clicked photographs of us. She had them printed in the next town, and gave them to us one day. We didn't know what to make of it – most of the young ones who visited took photos of us to keep for themselves, to look at us when they were far away. In the photos, we stood on the dirt tracks doing nothing but smiling, hands hanging uselessly at our sides. It made us look lazy and jobless, like we were louts. Still, there was something captivating about holding a photograph in our hands. Some of us placed the photos in our houses, next to the painted calendar of the gods. That way we understood the photos, the way they were cocooned in time while we aged looking at them. It gave us the idea to take a picture of Ray-chil, so we could put her in our houses too, forever. It made us excited, to be able to show others the beautiful white lady who came one day.

Ray-chil understood what we meant quickly enough, and with a big laugh that made her whole face go as red as Aruni's tomatoes, she agreed. She gave the camera to Mohan and stood under a tree, facing the sun. We started to pose with her – first Ramnath, then Gopi, and then Prasad. Some of us who were passing by realised what was happening, and began to line up for the same opportunity. Nandu did his part by spreading the word even further, and bigger crowds began to form. Ray-chil was very nice about it all. She smiled, laughed, spoke a little bit in our language to encourage the shy ones among us. Mohan kept taking the photos. Women wanted to take part, then entire groups of children on their way back from school. Time passed, the day grew long. Ray-chil never stopped, never said no. In fact, we noticed a glow come to her face, a strange kind of breathlessness that came over her as we lavished our attention, as we let her know we wanted a piece of her to be with us forever. She seemed to know it, drink in our yearning with her eyes, aware of a yearning of her own. Our crowds, our easy spotlight on her gleaming skin, seemed to feed her.

We think Mohan noticed too. After some time he seemed to slow down, taking the photos in a more lackadaisical manner, as if his heart was not in it. Many times he suggested they stop for the day, but Ray-chil would goad him on, saying he should not disappoint his fellow villagers. She ignored Mohan's retort that he cared more for her health than the villagers' disappointment. "Oh, but they like looking at me," Ray-chil said, and we agreed with her. After a while Mohan no longer met Ray-chil's eyes, and finally when dusk came, Mohan abruptly shut off the camera, picked up his bags and started towards Velan's house, leaving Ray-chil with Balu the blacksmith.

Nandu managed to eat breakfast at Velan's house the next day, showing up unannounced with a hungry grin that Ammani Mami recognised, letting him in with a swat on his head. He said things were different. Ray-chil sat down on the floor with Velan and Mohan, trying to cross her legs the way they did, but "unable to stay that way for long. Mohan showed her how to use her hands to smash up the *idlis*, to dip it into the chutney before bringing it to her mouth. Velan told Mohan he thought Ray-chil did do it well – perhaps she lacked some grace, but there is no use being fussy over the little details with someone who hasn't been brought up in our ways. He wasn't about to tell her that in small places like this the men ate first, and that women were to wait till after – things are changing; we must change with them.

But after Mohan finished and left to wash his hands, with bits of *idli* and *sambhar* running down his palm, Ray-chil barely picked at her breakfast.

Mohan came more often to the riverside, to bathe with Velan and other men from the village. He grinned more fully, like the young Mohan we knew. His lips stretched right to his ears, showing us all of his thirty-two teeth. He did not have Ray-chil with him. We saw her at different times, in different places, with her camera, taking pictures of us while we bent our backs to plant our paddy. Since that day when some of us were able to take photos with her, word had spread through Nandu and some others, and Ray-chil received a lot of requests. No matter where she went, there would be someone who had missed out that day and wanted another chance. Some of us even dared to say we wouldn't mind having a second picture taken with her – after all, we said, she looked so different in anything she wore. Ray-chil seemed pleased with our compliments, but felt there were too many of us, and too little time – she and Mohan were leaving in a few days. Nandu then had the brilliant idea of organising a single day where we could all wait in line and take photos with her. It would be a special occasion. Ray-chil seemed pleased, and said for that occasion she would wear something Indian.

We saw her visit our local tailor, who was so honoured by her visit he insisted she stay and have something to eat in his house, cooked by his wife. Many of us loitered around outside while she was with the tailor, and surely some of the young men wished they were the tailor instead, taking her measurements. At times like this we forgot Ray-chil was married, and to this day cannot recollect Mohan's presence during these preparations.

On the day, we dressed up as best as we could, as if it were a festival at the temple. We wore our best silks, and brought out our best gold, and obtained the freshest jasmine and orange *kanakambaram* flowers for our hair, the cleanest shirts and *veshtis*. We gathered around to wait for Mohan and Ray-chil.

We waited for nearly three hours. They never came.

Nandu said it might have been his fault, although he was not very sure. He had been sent to Mohan's family orchard, with the mission of delivering some of Ammani Mami's jewellery to Ray-chil. He had run as fast as he could, and when he arrived at the orchard, filled with mango and guava trees, he saw Mohan and Velan in the water tank, stripped to their shorts and frolicking like little boys just off school. Ray-chil had come up to them, in the tailor's sari and matching blouse. The tailor had really found the right colour for her, Nandu told us, such lovely maroon and sandalwood hues. He caught up with her just as Mohan spotted them, he said.

"You look beautiful," said Mohan, as Ray-chil strung on Ammani Mami's gold chains and bangles and dangling earrings. She stood close to the tank, occasionally dipping her hand into it to splash the back of her neck, a tip she had picked up from us to help with the heat.

"Thank you," said Ray-chil. Apparently she looked touched. "Do you like the bindi?"

"Yes, but here we call it *pottu*," said Mohan.

"Potu?"

"*Pottu*. Never mind. What's the occasion?" Nandu saw Ray-chil's face change at the question. Nandu found the conversation hard to follow, since he'd learnt English only through some extra classes and some American television. It all sounded like "das-bus" to him. But he knew enough to tell us nobody was going to win.

"The photos, don't you remember?"

"Of course I remember."

"No, you don't."

"You're going in that?"

"What's wrong with this? "They seem to like me in it." It was true, we told Nandu, that we liked it on her, because it made her stand out more, made her rise out of a flat background, like the curvy statues at the temple.

"Why do you always need to make a spectacle of yourself?" said Mohan, and Nandu said Ray-chil stood very still. Velan climbed out of the water tank, but neither husband nor wife looked in his direction.

"I'm already one," said Ray-chil, tilting her chin up.

"Then don't make it worse."

"Why is it worse? What's wrong with them liking me?"

Mohan didn't answer, and Ray-chil's eyes widened. "Oh my God. I can't believe this. You're jealous."

"Don't be ridiculous."

"Oh God, it's true!"

"You're being silly. Why on earth would I be jealous of my own people?"

Ray-chil looked triumphant. "And so they can't be my people. I'm only doing this for you – "

"You're doing this for yourself."

Apparently it was Ray-chil who first splashed the water onto Mohan. Mohan initially froze, mouth agape, and with a yell splashed his wife right back. She responded in kind, and Nandu started to laugh, thinking it was a game, the kind he played with his brothers when bathing in the river. The married couple laughed too, giggling and squealing in their wet frenzy. In a few seconds they both lost strength and subsided – Ray-chil took a step back from the tank and stared at her husband, as if sighting a peculiar animal. She then looked back at herself, her wet clothes, and sighed. Mohan's face collapsed momentarily, but before he could say anything, Ray-chil said in a flat voice Nandu hadn't heard before, "There, you got your way. There's no way I can pose for anything now. Happy?"

Some of us were loitering around Ammani Mami's house, despondent and full of questions, when Nandu informed us the photography session was cancelled. We were devastated. We thought it would be easy enough for

49

Ray-chil to change into something else, perhaps wear something of Ammani Mami's, or maybe even dry the sari and wear it another day. But it became clear nothing like that was going to happen, not anymore. There was a high amount of hustle and bustle in Ammani Mami's house, with only snippets of information leaking out about the married couple having to leave urgently. The word spread, and like the first time, the crowds swelled, wanting to say goodbye. Manickam, Balu, the milkman, even the Kali Amman priest came. Some of the younger ones burst into tears. Nandu, the little traitor, now that he was conscripted into helping the couple pack and shift their luggage into the Ambassador, suddenly behaved like their insider rather than ours, and refused to tell us anything.

We surged ahead as they came out of Ammani Mami's house for the last time, trying to catch a last glimpse. Velan and some other men pushed us back, deaf to our cries. Ray-chil and Mohan came out, carrying their luggage, and our pleas grew louder, our arms outstretched. She saw us and shrank back. We wanted to tell her we only wanted to talk to her, touch her one more time before they disappeared into their shiny world. She shielded herself behind Ammani Mami, almost like a child. Mohan hugged Velan, and Ray-chil put her palms together. Both of them squeezed into the Ambassador, which could barely move because of us. Ray-chil kept her eyes down, like a good Indian wife. Some say her eyes were red. Mohan spoke to us, called some of us by name, even smiled a little, but if we looked at him, it was to plead for a glance from his wife.

We waved at the dusty road as their Ambassador roared away, shouting "bye-bye, ta-ta!" like we had seen in our films. We kept waving much after they had turned the corner, still looking at the road, still thinking of Ray-chil. Though we understood, we felt bad. We felt somehow responsible. We had cut Nandu down to size just a few minutes before the couple came outside, and discovered from him that for about half an hour before Mohan and Ray-chil were to leave, Ray-chil had climbed up to the roof all by herself. He had been sent to fetch her so they wouldn't be late, and he had found her standing on Velan's patch. She had stood rigid, feet deeply embedded in the grass, looking down at the luxuriant carpet of almost artificial green. She had stayed that way for some time, despite Nandu's increasingly nervous calls, unseeing of anything but the grass. Nandu said she hadn't even blinked.

The Man With Two Wives

So I've been hearing you all call me the man with two wives. You jokers. What you know? You think I am like one of those fellers, keeping one on the side quiet-quiet while everybody laughs away? Or that I took my cue from the Malays, marrying two three times under Islam. I'm not like that okay. I have seen all you fellers do that. Some of you even go to prostitute, while the wife and daughter go to pray in Batu Caves. That is what I call cheap lah, not this. This I let the whole world know. No secrets one. For what want to keep secret? You all going to come help me when I sit in hospital dying is it? What is marriage, what is wedding? A big bunch of people come around, make a lot of noise, tie some strings together, be a witness to the fact that now this guy will be fucking this girl, and this girl will fuck nobody else. That is it. And for the sake of that kind of – what – *permission*, we spend so much of money, make nice food, print invitation, bring nadaswaram band, all that big hoo-ha. So?

So Lata is not my wife because I didn't have all this nonsense with her? You all won't look at her directly, when she go temple or do shopping, but once she turn around, you all start. Whispering-whispering. Ei, don't look at her lah, look at me. I'm the one who made the choice isn't it. She is more my wife than my first one lah. What, now you pitying the first one? Wondering how I have the heart to do this to that poor woman, who is always in selai, always with pottu, always going to temple-temple.

What do you know about my home life? What do you know about what I become in that house? How before saying five sentences I want to hold my head and scream at the walls because I feel I'm being dragged back into the darkness I came from?

Look, how long have we been here? I mean us, lah, people like us – no, not fifty years lah, that one since independence only, I'm talking from those days. Can you remember how we all came to be here? My father ran away from his house in Madras, he was only seventeen then you know. He got on the steamer and straight landed in Penang. Never looked back. I don't know how, all I know, in primary school, he had twelve makan shops, all over Penang. It was almost half of Gurney Drive. An uncle once took me around, showing me all the shops as he carried me on his shoulders. He point-point and said "This one your father's, this one your father's, this one also your father's." So of course lah I thought, one day it will all be mine, isn't it, so what for I want to break my arse and study in school?

The darkness started in secondary school – all I remember is we had nothing. If I came back home wet after jumping into the river, sure will get rotan from the big man. Nicely he used to give, on the backside. "How many times I told you," he would ask. "How many times, not to jump in the river? I come home, and this is what I see? Bloody stupid buggers!" He was only beating us because he had been drinking his samsu, because the man's business was going, and he was taking it out on us. But how to realise that at that age? My mother, all she did was cry, look a bit scared, and then give some extra fish later with the rice. But she didn't ask the man to stop his hitting – not once, machan.

Ei, hello, are you listening? You think I talking to the wall ah? I'm saying no matter what happened, no matter where we come from, at some point, we have to start again from somewhere, isn't it, we have to start again from zero. I had to go to school again, while the big man was still going on his samsu. How much I studied, you also don't know. You know that story about Abraham Lincoln, how he studied under street lights? Oi, that story they take from us one lah. You know how many kerosene lamps I had to burn every night to study – sometimes I had to hide from my father, not like he understood what the hell was going on. Well, no shame in saying this, but I had to sit for my exams a few times. What to do, I had to study by myself, too old for school by then. But in the end I got through lah, and I got through well.

After that, you would think things would brighten, right? Want to go to university, do application all. But you know how my mother and brothers and I trembled thinking of the application itself? All those certificates, all those recommendations. We living in papan house, with electricity going so often, this world of papers was a scary one. My father did one great thing I'll always remember. He went to a Chinese towkay we knew, to talk to him about getting a reference letter for me. I had helped the man sometimes, carrying his letters to post to Hong Kong. That man also is a nice man, he wrote a very nice letter, in full English, like from the British like that. I read it out to everyone in the house that night, and they all thought I must be so intelligent, to read English so properly.

And then of course you know the rest. We all have different versions of this story, isn't it – with all my marks, all my papers, all the recommendations, nothing happens. Why? Because no place for me. There's place for all those naataans, the bloody Malays, who get in even with Grade 3. Sometimes there is not a single A in the result list. But they must get in what, got quota for them what. But me, and the Chinese fellers, and the other Indian fellers, with all those As, no, sorry ah, no place for you, thank you very much, see you later. And then these days, with my daughter finishing Form Five, people wondering why the country in such a bad state. I tell you.

So then, I get into business lah. Find proper job, as they say. And how many jobs? Wah, if you hear the list means sure you pengsan one. Plumbing. Electrician. Cooking in mamak stall. Carpenter making furniture. All kinds lah. Then I realised, no matter what job, no matter how educated you are, at the end of the day, everybody needs money. And to make money, you must first put in money. So I decided to do the same thing, do the one thing we all know – I opened a masala shop.

Yes, that's how it all started – one small shop on China Street, and just that one machine, with the top like an open mouth looking up at the sky. When I first saw it, I knew this was the right thing for me. Sure enough, in six months I cover capital already, and then in two years I open second shop. See, that's why, wherever you are, if you stick to what you know, that's what will make you big. For the first time, I felt, this will be okay. I buy selai for my mother to wear, I buy medicine for my father, I send my brothers to school.

Around then lah, the marriage thing started. Started making money what, so suddenly must get wife. Got this girl lah, got that girl lah. People from this family, people from that family. Suddenly my mother had no other son but me. I tried explaining I wasn't interested. Too busy with the business. But then she went around the house with long face, and then later she complained her back paining, her chest paining. If I ignored her, sometimes she'll come back to normal, but then sometimes she won't eat dinner. Aiyo, when mother doesn't eat ah, especially when I making money like this, cannot lah. Serious man. I cannot take it. And she knows that. That's why all the sudden fasting, like Mahatma Gandhi only. You know, I'm sure ah, Gandhi also must have learnt this tactic from a woman.

So then I thought, okay lah, whatever lah, anything that will make her happy. I saw the wife for the first time at the wedding, and suddenly I felt like I had become an adult. Like suddenly I had *responsibility*. She sat next to me, by the fire, and repeated after the priest, chanting in Sanskrit. Really, at that point I thought, things could not get any better, that my father was right to run away and start again, could we have had this much happiness back in Madras? Of course, the man was at the back of the crowd, coughing like the world was ending, but looking at my bride I knew I had more to do, to get on with what he had started.

Sometimes when I go to my shops, and there's a naataan customer, somehow, I feel I never been to school, like that. Yes, they also come sometimes to buy my masala powder. I was selling them in nice packets, with a lingam chop on the top. It goes very fast, you know. The makciks and pakciks come asking for it specifically. But then, the way they talk to me, I tell you, as if I myself had just stepped off the ship, not my father. "Eh, Anney," they say, although I never feel like their elder brother, "Anney, semua ini berapa?" As if I don't know English. And then they look at me, and their eyes aren't even fully open, they are half-closed. Only a half look, like they don't have the energy to see me fully. And really, I don't know why, when they do that, I also feel like sometimes I'm not there. Only those times, I feel I see my skin, so black, like midnight before rain, no stars, and always those times I know there is something I want to say, but no idea what, and some more a bit – I don't know lah, what the right word is – not scared, that's too much, but a bit like – *dumbfounded* lah – yeah, like I have no words. If I say any words, they look at me like I am talking foren language, and I end up saying nonsense, so really all I can do is look somewhere else. So I do that also with these fellers, I look somewhere else.

That's how I started going to those night classes lah. Can study whatever you want – Engineering, Law, Accounting – and at night, when it's cooler. And now I have the money, so I can pay what. My English? I don't know, as long as I can write enough to pass lah. Even then, I decided Accounting lah. I know I'm good with numbers, numbers more than words, so stick with that, you know?

And you know what – the more I study, the more I like it. Like something becoming lighter inside. My mistake was in assuming everyone who didn't get education will appreciate it when they get it. See, the more I think, the more I want to tell the wife. I lie down in bed next to her, smelling the sambrani in her hair, and

I want to tell her about checks and balances, about how good it feels when after all the calculations everything ends up equal. There's something very satisfying about that, I tell you, to see that on paper. At least on paper. Then she would look at me, with her big big eyes, and I'm almost feeling she is going to cry, or hold me, and tell me she knows what I mean, and what do I hear? Tomorrow that Chetti feller will come, and we must go to that gold shop, they have new shipment from Madras, latest design. Aiyoh. Ei, you know how many times I tried ah. Many many ways you know. Take her to Cameron Highlands. Try to talk under the moon. Even try to write Tamil little bit little bit. Where got. Really like estate only. If I give her things she is all smiles, but if I want to give her my words, my thoughts, it's like I speaking foren language. Leceh you know, after a while. In studying only, I realise, life is not all about things. But how to explain to her – forget explaining – I cannot study also, with that sirukki forever asking things. Buy this lah, buy that lah, do this lah, do that lah. I feel like her servant sometimes. How to study properly in a house like that? Outside only all wearing saree, talking Tamil like a film actress, with all the words all pronounced properly, like have come from India itself. Everybody see means wah, they totally fall for it. Inside the house I only know. Okaylah, it's not like I treat her bad okay. I don't hit her, like some of you buggers do. But after work, and then classes, I must find time to study lah, you think my whole life is around Nalli's Silk Sarees is it? If I say anything, she'll only look at me like I had done something wrong. And then asking for money for more sarees, like there are no more sarees being made. At least when Malathi was born, she became distracted, and left me alone for a bit.

58

What, why you looking at me like that? Cannot say all this ah? Ya, we all have wife who cooks for us and say yes to everything in public means, must be all hunky-dory lah, cannot have problems one, how dare we have problems, right? To talk about not having love when there is a beautiful wife at home – goodness, cannot be real. Not good to say out loud, how lonely we can be. As long as it looks like I'm being looked after from outside, what is this nonsense of connection and all.

I still cannot remember where I first saw Lata. She says it was outside class one day, when it was raining, and apparently I was standing by the five-foot-way, under the awning, and holding my books close like they were my babies. Apparently I was the one who first spoke to her – I actually don't remember, if she wants to say that, it's up to her lah. All I know, suddenly, after class, she will be there, by the five-foot-way. Not that I paid attention. But then, after few days, one day she wasn't there. I look around also, cannot find. Turn here, turn there, nothing. Then I also start wondering, why I want to know so much where she is. Then next day I saw her, then yes lah, had to ask her, "Yesterday didn't see you, what happen?" I simply ask only, wasn't thinking anything, but then her eyebrows went up, her eyes widen a bit, and for a minute I thought I gone case, she going to think I some kind of cheap feller, but then she smiled. Fuyoh, I tell you. No make-up, no nothing on her face, but just like that, it was like one whole Chulia Street got hit by lightning. Then only I know, why all my classmates used to run like dogs to the cinema, to watch this Tamil padam, that Tamil padam. I thought they were all stupid – how I know, it happens like that only, when you're not looking for it, it comes like a natural disaster, no control one.

What, you think I suddenly romantic-romantic, after one smile? Like that means you know how many girls would have made me pokai by now. No lah, Lata not like that. When I first spoke to her, soon enough I realise, she is different, very intelligent. For one, real speaking. When she speak English ah, like Mat Salleh only. Not like me. The sentences all proper-proper, arranged nicely, as if put together by somebody else. "I thought you digested Hitchens very well," she said one time, and I thought she was talking about the lunch we had just had before. And every time she said "highly liquid investments", I would listen closely – the way she said the "k" in "liquid", and "v" in "investments" – I dunno lah, like I also turn liquid lah, ha ha ha. It was just so clear, the way she said it, like she can cut through the grey fog in my head. And when I open my mouth, even though I sound stupid, somehow I can tell her everything. Father, school, shop, Accounting. All. Even about the naattaan. And she will listen, like everybody else not there. She will lean forward, and her eyes go narrow, and then if something really serious, her lips will press down a bit. That's it. But it's like, I dunno, I feel so clean afterwards, like I just had full bath in kampung river. So cooling. Of course then at some point I realise it is time for me to go home, to wife and Malathi, and then wah, feet very heavy one.

Ah? When she found out I married! Aiyo, firstly, you must understand, I not the kind to go give sob story okay, I've seen you all do the same, sometimes rehearse in the car some more. This one accident lah, Lata somehow found my address, landed up in the house one day to surprise me.

You know, it's the only time when making a fool of myself didn't matter. I did dangerous things like bringing her to my masala shop, even though I knew all the workers would talk later. Wah, and did they stare at her. Such elegance, such grace, wasted on those black pigs. I sensed her watching me as I explained my plans for Lingam masala to her. Even though I babbled on about expanding about contacting supermarkets in Penang, and in two years supermarkets in Ipoh and KL, I could see she wasn't bored by it – she watched me, quietly, with – how the Mat Salleh say – a certain kind of *regard*. Usually after classes we will discuss our assignments, our difficulties – I usually ask her about the words in the textbook, she like a walking dictionary what. In exchange she would request my assignments, ask me about balancing assets and liabilities – and again her face will get that look while I explain to her what is so clear in my mind, the way numbers flow. I wasn't sure what that look was – I had never seen it before – until she once took me home to meet her mother. When the mother realised I was studying with her, she asked how much I earned, that Lata would make a great wife, knew how to cook all. Lata had to interrupt to shut her up.

"Don't mind her," she told me. "She's always trying to marry me off."

"And what is wrong with that?" the mother went off. "You and all your studying – how many men do you think are out there who would want a wife who knows more than them? Every man wants a woman who will be on his side, not someone who will understand what he says enough to disagree with him!"

"I'm not quitting the classes," said Lata, with that clip-clip tones the Mat Salleh make like this is final. But I saw her sigh. And she looked up, and her face changed when she noticed me. I don't know what expression I had, but I felt something weird, like I realised what her looks before meant. They had been looks of recognition, like when you're on a fairground with a crowd of strangers, a family member with features like yours pops into your vision. And I think that's what Lata saw on my face when she spoke to her mother.

So when she feels that comfortable, of course lah, she felt familiar enough to want to surprise me. Shows how much she had trusted me, aiyoh. I was in the shop, found out only when I went home. Apparently the wife had opened the door and seen Lata. And Lata, smart woman, had put everything together, and then left, quiet, dignified. Finish lah. When I got home, like World War Three, Four and Five had happened. I want to explain also, what words to use? Like there is this big fence around me – long time already anyway. So went to Lata to explain – ah, no, not explain, with Lata, straight, no thinking, go down on my knees. You don't look at me like that, if you are sitting there thinking what kind of man I am, not acting proper macho one, then you bloody feller, you have never felt it, you have not seen that lightning. And she? She scream, she cry, she throw things at me. I can only kneel in front of her, wrap my arms around her waist, and cry back.

So then yes lah, that's when I became that type, the one you see in the Tamil padam, bring flower lah, bring chocolate lah, bring movies lah. Prove to her I serious. Initially she refused to see me – pretended I was invisible during classes. Aiyah, that hurt like nothing else man, one thing to see it from the naataan, another thing to see it from her. But then slowly-slowly, I would get that *recognition* look from her again, when I answer question in class, when the lecturer announced my marks in class. And I not taking chance, man. Anything she want, I do. No complaints, no questions. She asked if I would leave my wife. What to argue! I would leave her any day! But then Malathi, different story lah. That girl studies like it's her hobby, not something she has to do. How to break her childhood? I tried bringing her out with me, getting her to meet Lata, see if they will get along. Lata at first was a bit hesitant, then she melted. "Oh, she looks exactly like you," she would say, and give Malathi chocolates. But Malathi would refuse, saying her mother didn't allow her to take things from strangers. Even me, she didn't listen to. I know this is the wife's work. That mother-daughter one team, I got no say one. Sometimes I enter a room they're in, and they would stop their conversation, and I know she's been talking about me, about Lata. What poison she's been pouring into Malathi's ears, God only knows. But it's very effective, more effective than her sobs and screams. Those sounds I can walk away from, but my daughter hating Lata ensures I have to be at a standstill. So all I could do was go to work, then go to classes, and study. Study like Malathi.

But my time all with Lata lah. Talking to her so much, I feel like my brain pushing everything together. Like its being put through my masala machine, have no idea what will come out of my mouth. And as if the more it gets squeezed, the more it expands, like the green sponge my mother uses to wash the dishes.

"Perhaps you should go for this interview," Lata said once, giving me a newspaper article. Accountancy job, big firm. I was a bit surprised, but of course I didn't show it. My chest started to expand. So much faith she had in me. Some more had finished our last paper only two weeks ago. "Just give it a try, they'll know the results won't be out for a while anyway." And I know she must be thinking, if maybe I get better job, I will have guts to divorce the wife.

And I went lah, because I thought she might be right. Woke up that morning, put on shirt-pant-tie, wah, like businessman like that. A real one. The wife bring me coffee, her mouth also open, like she cannot believe what she seeing. She then said "Do a small prayer to Lord Murugan before you go," I only kissed Malathi big time on the cheek, and then went off.

The office building ah, I passed many times before. It faced the sea. In fact I've seen some of my cousins in there sometimes, late at night, cleaning the marble floors. Sometimes I walk past it one the way to see Lata, and if they see me they will call out and we will chat for a few minutes. One of them, Karumari, she has blisters all over her feet, so she likes working there. She cannot wear shoes, they hurt too much, so she likes the marble, it's cooling. She would tell me this, and she would laugh, so loud, and it would echo off the walls. I would laugh with her. For some reason, don't know why, Karumari only coming to my mind, as I enter the lift, and press the button to the twenty-seventh floor.

The boardroom was like something out of one English movie lah. Fuyoh. Full carpet, thick-thick curtains all. The interviewers, four people man! Four people to talk to one person! All wearing suit, memang pun they need one, inside so cold. The whole thing enough to cekik you, so much fabric everywhere, like cannot breathe, seriously.

I went in, shook hands with all of them, sat down. My ears like have the whole Indian Ocean inside, roaring, whoosh-whoosh. First question, can answer. Second question, also can answer. The board members all naattaan one, except for the one main guy – wei, Mat Salleh you know. He was in the middle, bigger than two

64

of the naattaans put together, and he was the only one
who smiled. So funny, although he is the white one –
actually, fair to say, pink one lah – he's the one who
seemed most friendly – like he cannot see what the rest
of them see. Or actually I should say – he see more than
the others. Because why? When the other two start the
third question, same thing. That look, they give me. The
half-look, eyes down, not really looking at me, like I am
not really there. Like they talking to some empty chair.
Exactly, I tell you. So exactly the same, until I have to
look down, check myself, see if I'm wearing the shirt-tie,
or whether I'm in my usual banian, sweating and
shouting at the masala shop. I want to open my mouth
to answer also, air only come out. I so afraid I'm going to
say things like, "Adei, enna, jintan manis one packet, fish
curry powder three packets, where the turmeric lah?"
Aiyyo, I don't know what they said after that. I look
down, and yeah, like really I wearing my banian, and my
skin so black, I think of Lata, I think of how she talks,
how I talk when I with her, how my words will tumble
out like a Gunung Jerai waterfall, falling everywhere,
coming out of every thought. But no, skin still black,
tongue still one bloody big piece of metal. All the
Accounting, all the numbers, all the classes, all the books
– for what I also don't know. The son of that stupid guy
who lost all his money what. I was sure they could see it,
they could see it on my skin, those fucking naattaans
with eyes half-closed.

You know, it's funny, I was thinking of Lata the whole
time, what she would say, how she would react. I was
walking thinking of her, in my mind, hoping she won't
be disappointed, and then somehow, I end up home. My
wife saw me, I don't know what was on my face that she
saw, she ran out like she had seen her own father or

Murugan Himself. Me, I don't know, my eyes watery, I knew I walking like I mabuk with five beers or something, and I was trying to take off the tie, I didn't know why it was there still, because supposedly I'm in banian, and then I was on the floor, my knees gone, and I'm holding my wife, and she is holding me up, but I don't know if it is my wife or Lata, and I'm crying, crying, crying like small baby got no milk. And Malathi there, in a corner, holding a mug of Milo, I know, she is seeing me, she is seeing this, and she is wondering what is happening.

Lata was very nice about it all. As usual, she listened, as I stuttered and stammered, trying to explain the interview to her while she drank her teh tarik at the mamak stall. I just said lah, that they cannot offer me anything until they knew the results themselves, fair only what. I don't know what made her react, maybe my tone, at one point she just leaned over the table and put her hand over mine. By now people in the mamak stall sure we two married one. She just said "Never mind, don't worry, there's always a next time." Thing is, her lips press down this time very hard, and for a long time some more, so I don't know what that means, but still, somehow, I had to tell her, "Lata, my sweetheart, no, I don't think I can go for another one."

Ei, seriously lah. I cannot have Malathi seeing this, that girl ah, you won't believe it, her brains sometimes go off like a rocket, I think even Lata will kalah next to her. She come back from school, all first in the class one. Highest marks, always. She never thinks of things like jumping into rivers or how much money her father makes. Best thing what, this is how it should be. What for she should see her father behaving like an idiot, crying like a stupid man. She deserves better isn't it.

66

Somehow I cannot tell Lata this, very weird you know. Just like I cannot tell her what really happened at the interview. She of course passed with flying colours, and in like two months got job already, junior auditor. No surprises isn't it. Me, after all our discussions, as usual, in the exam, the English all over the place, habis lah. But scraped through in the end, okay lah. I don't know if she suspects anything on my part lah – one thing she knows, she has me around her little finger. Every time she call, sms, I'm out of my house, straight go to her. No questions asked. Ei, it's the least I can do lah. She has got one whole Penang against her because of me. I buy her one whole Thangamaligai gold shop also not enough. But these days...we still talk all, and I see her eyes will go somewhere else. Last time I go to her house when the mother not there – nowadays I must beg to be invited, and even then when I get there suddenly its like I'm there for the first time, so formal one. Once in a while she will bring up my Accountancy result, I look around only, and start talking something else. Cannot lah. What was I thinking. And then I would see Lata sigh, something she thinks I cannot understand. She doesn't know I see it ten times more in my wife.

Sometimes when Malathi used to talk about her maths homework, for some reason the wife will look at me, and her face will change a bit, and it will remind me also of something very weird, when she look like that, like a primary school teacher looking at boy who pee in class. She look so much like Lata, I have to get out of the room. And what's worse, that look will change to a different one. This look she keeps for like those cousins, the ones who clean those big offices, when they come visit, she speaks to them like that, with that gentle smile, her head turning a bit to the side, and nodding slowly-

slowly. This look was like the naattaan politicians tolerating the stupid journalists asking if Malay supremacy is legal. Wondering why they have to sit there and be bothered. I get that look too. Some days I cannot decide which look makes me want to vomit more. And then I think of that day lah, how she was holding me, yeah it really was her. You know, this is what wives do, and this is what the one you really love sometimes doesn't know she must do. Because she's so used to being the one being held, she doesn't realise sometimes she can do the holding as well, the holding that the wife does. I can still feel that hold, except that now I seem to remember it as something hard and sticky, like cannot pull away like that.

Right now all I know is Malathi. Her Form Five results coming out next month, but already the teachers all calling to congratulate her. Sure straight As one, they are saying. Top student. Get ready to answer phone calls from the papers, they will come to write articles about your daughter. When she bring her friends over and they speak English, wah, I can barely even understand. Some got accent some more, like from New York like that. And her friends ah, I lost count already what name and where from lah. Malay name, Chinese name, Indian name, even some Eurasian-Eurasian ones, all fair-fair. And she talk to them all like biasa only. You see lah, when she finish university ah, when she go for job interview, sure no problem one. She will talk the pants off that Mat Salleh feller, the naattaan feller will be staring only, eyes wide because of how good she is. That is how it will be, man. She won't have to go looking for people to talk to, they will all come to her. Only thing, since past two years, sometimes some boys will also come with her friends. Also all speaking-speaking like born in London. They all chat-chat, say, "Hi uncle, how are you uncle" to me, then nicely she takes them to her room! I turn around to the wife, she always ready, looking at me steady. No blinking. Whatever words I had also, all disappeared.

Oi, why you now so quiet lah? Don't worry man. I have my masala shops lah. Last year, two more open, on the other side of Penang. So now, twenty in all. I now go to the shops everyday, wearing my blue banian, my favourite. When I smell the powders so much that I cough, when I hear the noise the machines make with the spices, like the Penang monsoon thunder, I wonder why I even bothered with stupid numbers. I already made, man. Anyone ask means, they all point to me, they all know me. No shame. And then they say lah, as you all know, that man ah, he got two wives one. One in the house, one he keep somewhere else.

I.C.

Already forty minutes, and we were not moving. It's not like I hadn't warned her, but no, she would have none of it, I could see just by that tilt of her chin. "Keep to Jalan 16/11," she had said, right? Even though I had been saying there would be such terrible traffic there at this hour, especially with Chinese New Year. But you know I value my duty, my son, so if she is willing to pay my meter charge extra one-and-a-half hour, I will not complain. At least we could keep talking.

"Ei, very hot ah, today," she said. I turned up the air-conditioning so it would reach her in the back, like I do for all my customers. I was not like those idiots who stayed in the shell of their thoughts their whole working day. People can be very interesting, if you only let them show you how.

"Now, cooler?" I asked. It was an innocuous enough comment, something to restart the conversation she had abruptly halted. Pretend like it never happened, and maybe we could start again.

"Hmm." The rear-view mirror showed me glimpses of the things I didn't pick up at first – a furrowed brow, a flash of silk, make-up melting on her shiny skin. Whatever she was, she was definitely city folk, from the way her nails were done.

"Going back from work, ah, girl?"

"Yes."

"How come you're not taking the LRT?"

"Very crowded lah, this time. I have to stop by and buy some nasi kandar some more."

This time I listened with the intensity of a surgeon picking up information on a patient's vitals. What's in that accent? Too polished, but just enough edges to tell me she's not from KL proper. Nice English, but not like those in business. A little bit proper, a little bit not. It told me nothing.

On purpose, I thought suddenly, but I dismissed it. No, Kathiresan, don't get paranoid. There is no reason for her to be dishonest with you.

"Oh, you didn't tell me that. You have another stop?"

"No, no, if uncle can stop at the pasar malam in Jalan Ampang first, then later quickly drop me in SS 2, it should be fine."

"Meter will still be running you know."

"Yeah, what to do, the in-laws are coming tomorrow, I must make something nice."

I shifted in my seat, looking away like I was trying to avoid bad news. We had only been through two red lights, despite my weaving and cutting. Well, this time she was the one making the personal remark. What does that prove? It's not like I had brought it up, I didn't breach anything, my son.

Normally this would never be such a problem. In the twenty odd years that I have been doing this, more often than not a good chat is the best way to deal with KL traffic. Rain or shine, floods or tolls, when there is someone there in the moving box with you, time passes with enough pleasantness that sometimes I forget who is supposed to be taking whom. You know how many people I meet! American businessmen, Chinese prostitutes, Syariah Court lawyers, Malay housewives, sometimes even some Indian doctors going for night duty. You would think that having so many different kinds of people in my taxi would mean I learn a lot from them. At one point, that was true, but you know, these days, I know so much that most of the time I'm the one giving everyone advice. I told the Malay housewife the best hospital to take her baby son for his vaccinations, I told the Chinese prostitutes which areas get patrolled at night, and I told the American feller to be adventurous and go eat at a Kampung Baru kopitiam. Okay, so, the last one I did for fun, but you know, he would have had an experience not many tourists get to have, even if he ends up on his five-star hotel toilet at the end of the day.

And it is such a nice thing, to tell people what they need to know, sometimes even without them asking, sometimes even without them knowing. When I lie in bed waiting for sleep to come, once in a while I would think on what all happened that day, and how I was able to tell people things. Of course, you always had those who would get in, bark a destination then go quiet like a corpse. That was in the olden days, when you could zip around KL like a quick pinball game. And then when the traffic jams started, and the flash floods, and we all had no choice but to sit in front and behind a thousand other cars all day and all night, more people started talking. And they talked of things that I know they wouldn't tell their closest friends. Those days I would get shocked by things like young university girls telling me about their period.

"What times we live in, nothing is private anymore," I would think, as I dropped them off to big, beautiful, air-conditioned malls. They would lightly hop off, perfectly coiffed, all ready to spend their fathers' money. But then when the handphone came in the 90s, the meaning of even that privacy was not the same anymore. Again people didn't really talk in the taxi, but that was because they were too busy showing off by calling their whole family on the big black handphone. By the time I got myself one, everyone was on SMS, so now they boasted by not shouting but beeping.

But still, whether they wanted to talk or not, beep or not, phone or not, I would normally know within ten minutes of being in the taxi. If no talking I turn to my radio, if I like the look of the customer, I will even change it to a station I think they may like. So for the Chinese I put One FM, the Malays I put ERA, otherwise if it is *makkal*, one of us, I let it be at THR Raaga. For the tourists, of course, I put on Mix FM, although mainly I cannot stand the stupid noise from it.

But then this one, this girl here, sitting not smugly but not nicely, with skin that seems to get golden when the sunlight hits her, with her, I cannot seem to know whether we are to speak or not. It's not like I didn't try. It's not like she never responded. But for some reason with her I'm all at sea again, I'm floating without a proper anchor, and I cannot find a way in. It's like those days again, those very olden days before all the traffic, when it was just kampung and factories and muddy rivers, and my mind was a dark velvet sheet.

If anyone asked Kathi what he wanted to be when he grew up, he would say "the best marble player in the world". The adults would all chuckle and brush his mop of hair with loving indulgence. Sometimes visitors brought marbles with them as little gifts.

73

He had about 22 marbles with him, and would challenge anyone to a game at the mere mention of it. With his white singlet that he rarely changed out of, Kathi would be out of his school, into his house for a quick bite of sambal fried fish, and out again before his father had registered his presence. He would run barefoot on hot laterite, passing dozens of houses built like matchboxes with eyes and mouths, and head straight towards the coconut grove, where he knew the other boys were waiting. His mother screamed at him every time – he realised the quicker he left, the less he had to hear it.

Ei, its Kathi, Kathi is here, they would say when he showed up, pockets bulging. He would lead them into the selected clearing, make a head count, and proceed carefully to arrange his marbles together, to form a tight circle right at the centre, in full view of everyone. He was always very slow and deliberate about this, examining each marble for flaws before placing it gingerly down. This was very serious business.

He would then take his biggest marble, and fling it strategically to break the circle, and the game would start. "Pick one", he would say, and Ah Liong or Balan or Hanif would point to a hard to get piece – a beautiful taupe, or an aubergine, or a magenta – and Kathi would screw his face, one eye shut, tongue out, and make a hit.

By the time he returned home, it would be dark, and his mother would be lighting the kerosene lamp out on the front as he slipped past, demanding to be fed. Rice, salted fish, chillies. He would eat on the linoleum floor and eavesdrop on the radio programme his father dutifully followed in the living room, the happiest boy on earth.

One day, during such a meal after a ravenous run

back home, Kathi's Appa bustled into the kitchen where he sat, slightly breathless and eyes bulging, as if he'd run all the way from the neighbourhood temple. "Are you listening to this?" he asked Amma, and then to his mother, Kathi's grandmother, who sat at the back of the house, out of everyone's way.

"Ennanga aachu?" asked Amma, and Kathi saw her raspy voice and her lazy pronunciation change the look on his father's face, interrupting something more important. "The whole world will collapse around you as you sit there and just feed your son," he said. "Don't care about the rest of the world, just stay there." Which of course meant they had to follow him. They shuffled out of the kitchen, even Kathi's grandmother, into the living room, and settled around the green and purple carpet, facing the polished wooden radio taking up centre stage like a deity in a sanctum.

"Aiyo, my legs are hurting me, must you do this to me in my old age?" creaked grandmother.

"Kathi, take your plate with you, if you leave it in the kitchen the next door cat might come in and start having it," said Amma.

"Ssshh, ssshh, listen, lah, listen, listen," said Appa.

"*I am indeed proud that on this, the greatest day in Malaya's history, it falls to my lot to proclaim the formal independence of this country. Today as a new page is turned, and Malaya steps forward to take her rightful place as a free and independent partner in the great community of Nations, a new nation is born and though we fully realise that difficulties and problems lie ahead, we are confident that, with the blessing of God, these difficulties will be overcome and that today's events, down the avenues of history, will be our inspiration and our guide.*"

The family had been leaning toward the radio, to catch every word. Appa, a mountain of authority standing upright closest to the contraption, nodded his head gravely at every pause, so that Kathi could no longer tell if his father was listening to the news as something received from the outside, or whether he was somehow responsible for making it happen in the first place.

Appa turned around to his family with deliberate force, sweeping his tree-trunk arms with a sense of triumph, like MGR had done in *Adimai Penn* the week before at the city cinema hall. "My darlings," he said, with uncharacteristic affection, "it is almost done. We are nearly there. After more than two hundred years, ten years after Madras, this will finally be a free country." He closed his eyes to savour the moment.

"Why wasn't it free before?" asked Kathi.

Appa opened his eyes and grunted. "Because of useless fellows like you, running off to play marbles instead of doing your homework," he said, and sat heavily into his rattan chair.

"Why scold your son like that?" said Amma, when the boy began to cry.

"Because he needs to know what he is going to inherit. Finally, there will be no more vellaikaaran Tuan for us to tabik all the time as he passes by. What did they do when the Jappaan feller came? You remember or not? If I hadn't been their chapkang, teaching Nippon Go in their schools, you think you could have given milk to this one here? It's about time lah. We did okay when they weren't here for a while, we can do okay when they are permanently not here." And with that Appa settled back into his sofa, to listen to the songs from Sivaji and MGR movies.

And so Kathi had a new game to play when he went to the coconut grove after school. Ah Liong, Balan and Hanif and him would get together, and they would find long, sturdy twigs they labelled guns. They would make quick, whispered plans in a huddle, and then march around with solemn looks on their faces, yelling "Merdeka! Merdeka!" to the burning blue sky watching over them as they brandished their weapons. Ah Liong was usually the loudest, and he seemed to really feel it, too, and he told them, that his elder brother had gone missing during the Japanese time, that his father was getting thinner and thinner trying to find him, and that the Mat Salleh could not care less about it. "We can eat shit, lah, it doesn't matter to them," said Ah Liong, and everyone grew quiet. Ah Liong could say words like that, with the proper effect and emphasis, like he had been privy to experiences that allowed, even required, such words. Hanif brought pieces of old newspapers, and would read it out, sitting with one leg over the other like his father. He could only say a few words from any of the articles, and not very fluently, so to make up he would read all the words he knew from all the articles, so that sometimes reports of roundtable conferences in London seemed to have dancing joget girls entertaining the proposed clauses of free speech because of new imams wanted in a mosque where there was going to be continuous rain for the next five days.

"Eh, your newspaper a bit odd, lah," said Ah Liong. "Where got rain in one mosque one."

"Why? How you know? You can't read Jawi, right?" said Hanif quickly.

"No, lah, but at least I know when it rains it rains everywhere."

"You never know. Sometimes miracles happen,

especially if you have faith. Maybe that's why it is in the paper."

The boys could not dispute that.

Usually when my customers get inside my taxi, my son, it's the eyes I first notice. One can understand so much from them so quickly, whether they're tired, happy, stressed, even if they might be good or bad people. I once had a passenger who turned up in the news the next day as a wanted murderer. I knew there was something off about him, not because he didn't want to talk, or that he fidgeted constantly, but because his eyes were just so blank. He said it was his first time in Kuala Lumpur, but he didn't really seem to be enjoying the sights of the highrise buildings by the road. He looked at everything with a Robocop gaze, like he saw no meaning in them. So somehow I wasn't so surprised.

With this girl, when she opened the back door of the taxi and asked me to take her to SS 2, it was her hands I registered first. They were long and slender, but had pronounced knuckles, with lines etched deeply at the joints. As she sat inside, with her office skirt and silk batik blouse, the word "toffee" came to my head. I pulled out into traffic, thinking, husband, big house, but no children yet.

Of course, it was 5.30pm, and KL traffic was doing its worst. More so, the skies had darkened, and the humidity shot up, and I knew once the rain started, I would be stuck with the one passenger all afternoon.

I glanced up at the rear-view mirror. She was looking out the window, not on the phone, not even a magazine.

"Where you from, girl?" I asked, just to help pass the time. The women were always nice and chatty.

"Around here, lah," she said. I looked up at the mirror

again, trying to place her. Her skin was wheatish brown, the kind the Malays had, but her features were more rounded, less flat and edgy. She was definitely not Chinese, although there was a tinge of yellow undertone. Best to ask.

"You Melayu ke?"

I noticed the eyes more closely, my son, as she flashed them at me, as if I'd asked something forbidden.

"Why?"

"Eh, don't worry, don't worry, I very broadminded, its not like I'm going to tell anyone you not wearing tudung," I replied in all honesty.

"I have no need to cover my head, pakcik," she said, and went quiet again. I wondered what she meant. Did she mean she was a non-practising Muslim kind of Malay, or just the uncaring urban kind of Malay, or just not Malay?

"Oh, so then you mix, ah? Cannot be Chinese, your eyes so nice and big," and I laughed good-naturedly, trying to put her at ease. She didn't respond. I stopped laughing, and took a quick turn at a traffic light, remembering a shortcut in the area. The traffic cleared out temporarily, and I made the most of it, while ticking off a list in my head.

"Ahhh, you must be Chindian, ah," I ventured.

"No, lah."

"Peranakan?" I couldn't really detect any old mixed blood in her appearance, I was just guessing.

"Aiyo, no lah."

"Not Nyonya Baba also ah?"

She exhaled. "Why so important one, uncle?"

I was certain by now of the mixed blood. It at least explained her reluctance to the simplest question anyone in KL ever asked anyone else in polite conversation.

There was really no need to be so defensive, I thought, mixed blood in KL was not a big thing, it was almost normal, almost to be expected. Some of them were stunners, especially some girls, some were unfortunate, like Chindians who got the mother's small eyes and father's dark skin. But there was usually nothing to hide about it.

"Oh! I know! You Serani!" I should've guessed the Portuguese influence earlier. An urban migrant from Melaka, not yet used to KL's accepting ways. No wonder she didn't want to say anything, especially not these days with people throwing bombs at churches.

She slapped the leather seat with those hands. "Uncle! Really lah! This is the limit! What does it matter what I am? Will it make a difference to the fare? To how fast you will go? Ah?"

"Aiyah, girl, not like that lah…"

"Not like what lah. All you need to know is I'm a paying customer and you're a taxi driver. I give some face because you elder doesn't mean I have to put up with all these personal questions, all this who are you what are you nonsense. If cannot means please stop the taxi, I can take a different one."

The skies opened up and the afternoon squall started. Pedestrians weaved across the roads, narrowly missing vehicles, holding up shiny grey UV umbrellas. There was obviously something quite wrong with the girl, but if I didn't get to PJ quickly enough I may not get a passenger on the way back, so I decided to say nothing, and it felt like I am being my wife, the way she sometimes sulked with me by not saying a word for days.

Kathi sensed it was an important day because even as he sat on the front wooden steps of his house, trying to see if there might be a lost marble under the house stilts, he saw people walking by, with a sense of rush and importance.

"Why don't you look at that sunrise instead?" said Amma, bringing some kanji to feed him. "So rare, that my son is up at this hour, while the rooster in Maimunah's house is crowing."

But Kathi's attention was all on the dirt floor under the house, hoping for a glint of glass, and it only shifted when his father was ready to leave.

"Are you ready?" Appa asked, standing stiff at the door in starched khaki pants and white shirt, with three pens in a neat row peeking out of his shirt pocket. Kathi nodded.

"Boy woke up so early this morning, all because you said you were taking him along today," said Kathi's mother. Instead of replying, Appa skipped down the steps and steadied his bicycle.

"Front or back?" he asked his son.

"Front!"

"Wait till I get on then."

"Just one more mouthful, da, Kathi!" Amma pleaded.

"Wah, Mr Ashok, taking the son along ah, today," said Ah Liong's father, ambling past the house in pants that competed with Appa's.

Appa laughed a laugh Kathi had never heard in the house. "Yes, Gaik Yen, it's good for the next generation to understand all this, they are going to inherit everything one day, isn't it." His voice boomed, making his words seem profound. Gaik Yen suitably nodded his head in agreement. "Yes, I've just come from there myself. It is a big day. Something to remember when talking to the grandkids, right?"

Kathi clung to the metal bar he straddled on the

bicycle, sitting in front of his father, and hunched over in the same manner as him. He still was not sure what the big day was, but the amount of people who flowed out of the houses on to the streets, like it was some sort of festival he hadn't been told about, confirmed that something was definitely going on. His repeated questions to his father had been met with stony silence, and so he now satisfied himself by observing the crowd, trying to keep steady so his father wouldn't lose balance of the bicycle, and counted all the marbles he had by memory.

They were on the bicycle for a long time, perhaps two hours or more. Kathi liked the silence between him and his father, and this sense of importance of going somewhere together to do something significant. Appa said nothing except some gentle grunts while cycling uphill, past rubber estates and pineapple orchards, along with other bicycles with other men. His breathing grew ragged, and Kathi gently tilted his head back so that it touched his father's chest. He could sense, through the shirt, through the sweat that mingled with his own when it trickled down the back of his neck, Appa's muffled heartbeat, and a sense of exertion that was beyond the physical, beyond merely trying to reach a destination. Kathi pressed in closer, inch by inch, imperceptibly. His father, hunched over him, large enough to seem like a canvas that could blot out the sun, reminded him of the limestone hills around the place, eternal and permanent.

Kathi guessed they were getting closer to their destination, because the laterite path had given way to a bigger, tar lane, which then had several other lanes coming to it, which then opened out to an even bigger lane. There were bicycles everywhere, even some motorcycles, and once there was a car that tried to make its way through by sounding a horribly loud horn, so that everyone had to stop to let it pass by. The buildings became bigger, the area noisier. Kathi had never been this far from home.

"This is it," said his father, stopping the bicycle by a street bicycle stand next to the biggest building on the street. A sign strapped across the rectangular body said National Registration Department. "This is where it starts, boy. This is the beginning of a new era."

Kathi had never seen this many people in one place before, not even at the temple for Deepavali, when people from all the neighbouring towns attended. Many of the side wooden doors of the brick building were open, with people streaming out in queues. Like Kathiresan and his father, they were dressed in freshly starched clothes that were beginning to soften from the humidity and sweat, as they stood patiently holding manila folders of precious documents.

Appa seemed to have a folder of his own. He held it close with one arm, and held Kathi's forearm with the other, leading him through the crowds with a firm grip. He looked up at the signs outside the doors and corridors, and Kathi followed him, pretending to be equally important on this very serious occasion, checking for signs that he could not yet read.

"Ah!" said Appa all of a sudden. "This is the one that is ours." The line stretched down the cement corridor, and down an open stairwell.

They found the end of the line, and stood patiently, waiting their turn. Kathi saw that everyone in front of them looked like him and his father, and everyone in another queue looked like Ah Liong and his father. Some way off, in the adjacent building, there were other queues, with people who looked like Hanif. They shuffled forward every few minutes, and Appa wiped Kathi's neck with his handkerchief every so often. Occasionally a wind would blow, and a stream of sighs would follow it, as people exhaled with temporary relief.

Kathi knew his father hated to wait. Everyone in the house had to be ready before he was, so he wouldn't have to wait once he had to leave the house. He once had to fetch Kathi from school, and because Kathi was late by two minutes in getting to the front gate, Appa had left. He had waited for Kathi to turn up at home after a long walk, and told him he had done this on purpose so that Kathi would learn the value of time.

The crowd inched along. Appa shifted his weight and looked around, looked ahead, looked everywhere. Finally he opened his manila folder, and showed its contents to his son.

"See, that, that one is for your mother," he said, holding a bunch of papers held together by a metal paperclip. The facing page had a picture of Amma, and two thumbprints. "This one," he continued, flipping to another set of papers, "is for grandmother."

He flipped more pages, and they shuffled forward a bit more. It seemed to help make time go faster.

"This, of course, is mine." Kathi saw a stern photograph of his father, unsmiling, and thought his moustache looked bigger than normal in it. His thumbprints were larger and darker than other members of the family.

"Is my paper also there?"

Appa frowned, and checked the pages of the documents. "Aah, let me see," he said, thumbing through them repeatedly.

"Oh!" he said finally. "Yours one is attached to your mother's."

"Why not one for myself? We are both men of the house after all."

Kathi never forgot the way his father laughed at that, throwing his head back, letting the laugh ring out without shame in that corridor of heat and whispers and shuffling.

"Of course, my son," he said. "Maybe they are waiting for you to be a bit older before you get your own one." He then bent down, eye-level with Kathi, and said, straight to his heart, "Until then, mine will be yours."

This time, when Kathi ran, it was as if his father was after him with a rotan. Pecut lari, a gunshot run from the house to the coconut grove, no room for questions. He'd show them this time. He had it safe in his pocket, folded over with good paper torn from his school notebook. He had had to wait till everyone was asleep before he took it, but he would put it back. It was his anyway, Appa had said so, even though the man refused when Kathi had asked outright if he could borrow the Identity Card.

"The IC," Hanif had said, with the seriousness that Ah Liong usually bore. It had seemed almost improper to Kathi, appropriating a heaviness that had been Ah Liong's birthright.

"So? I also went with my father to take IC," said Kathi. "But I still came here, right?"

Kathi's indignation then had come from having meticulously planned a good marble match, with nearly seven boys, and have only two appear at the clearing of the grove on the day. Hanif had been one of them, wearing a black songkok too large for his head. Kathi knew Hanif had a soft spot for his marbles. He'd play with his turquoise one for hours, turning it over on his fingers, mesmerised by its hue in the sun.

85

"Eh, it's important, lah, if the gomen come and we don't have IC, then they think you komunis and put you in jail. Or...worse."

Kathi wondered if Hanif was lying. The Identity Card had been a joyous, precious thing to obtain, something to cherish, not something to arm yourself with. When his father and he had finally reached the front desk, facing a yawning officer with droopy eyes smelling of soured milk, Appa had presented the Malay man with his folder. He had flourished it with the same pride he had shown on the night of the radio speech. Yet his voice was quite different – smaller, tentative, asking for permission.

"Identity Card application, sir."

"How many?"

"Three, sir. Myself, my wife and mother,"

"The boy?"

"With the mother, sir."

"Alright."

The man took out the papers from the manila folder and checked them with quick glances and impatient flicks. During the whole time, Appa stood ramrod straight, and Kathi checked the profile of his chest to see if it heaved with his breathing. It didn't.

"All in order," said the clerk eventually. "We will send you the IC in a few days,"

"Oh, thank you, sir," said Appa.

When the Identity Card finally arrived by post, Amma had placed all three of them on the home altar, in front of Mariamma and Pillayar, and Kathi's grandmother had spouted some mantras of blessing as he helped by ringing the small brass prayer bell in his hand. The cards had then been ceremoniously placed in a metal box, locked, placed on top of the cupboard in Appa's room, and the key placed in Amma's almari drawer.

"Nobody is going to put us in jail, lah," said Balan, the only other boy who had turned up for the marble meet. "It only means my father is citizen."

Hanif turned to Balan, a puzzled look on his face. "You also citizen? Eh, how can? Only bumiputera, lah, only the Malays."

"Eh, what nonsense, I also citizen, lah," said Kathi immediately. "I went with my father and took the IC, my whole family has it lah."

"Yes, lah, Hanif, you really like to make up stories, you know," said Balan, stepping away from Hanif towards Kathi. "Just like the raining in the mosque story. And Balan and Kathi laughed.

"I'm not lying! Don't be stupid! Look!" Hanif thrust his hand into the back pocket of his navy school shorts, and brought out the card itself. Balan, like Kathi, gasped. Hanif held it so casually, like it was money from his wallet, or a bus ticket. He held it like it was his own, and not just his father's.

"See, It says there. Kaum – bumiputera. That's me."

"That's your father lah," said Balan, though Kathi knew it came from envy.

"So? I my father's son, what. I also bumiputera."

Balan and Kathi weren't sure what to say to that.

"I also bumiputera," said Kathi.

"Don't lie," said Hanif.

"I'm not lying! You're a liar. Making up stories!"

"Shut up!"

Kathi hit Hanif, and the card flew to the ground with the boy. Hanif stood up and took a wild swing at Kathi, missed, and fell down again. Balan dived and found Hanif's Identity Card on the grass. He picked it up, blew on it, and stood looking at it for a few minutes before Hanif snatched it from him. "Give back to me!" he cried.

"Eh, don't be so perasan lah, I have my own card lah," said Balan, again walking backwards towards Kathi.

"So do I," said Kathi. "So don't act so big feller."

Hanif looked at the two of them, eyes nearly bulging with outrage. He then checked that the card wasn't damaged, before inserting it back in his pocket. "Ok," he said, in a manner unexpectedly limp. "Why don't you all then bring your ICs tomorrow. Then we can all look at it, and we'll know what it is for. And," he continued as an afterthought, "if people don't bring it, or don't have it, that means they are komunis," and he grinned.

"Of course, man!" said Kathi.

"Tomorrow," agreed Balan.

"Tell Ah Liong also," said Hanif. "Actually, I will tell him on the way back myself, I'm sure he's very proud to show it one."

The windscreen wiper creaked with annoying regularity. As we were not moving, I switched it off. I turned up the volume of the radio, set at THR Raaga, and quickly checked that it wasn't disturbing her. Her eyes were closed – she obviously wasn't in the hurry she had seemed to be earlier. I turned off the call radio so that it wouldn't disturb her. My taxi became quiet, a rare thing while I was on duty.

After ten minutes of fidgeting, I decided to SMS the wife at home. The Proton Wira in front was going so slowly I could drive with one elbow and three toes.

Tonight what dinner?

A few minutes passed before my phone beeped with an answer – *Why suddenly?*

Just asking lah.

There was no reply for a while, and as the lights had changed I decided to take a chance on them. I barely made it through, but it didn't matter because the gridlock continued.

"Aiyah, like permanent only," I said to myself.

The girl stirred in her sleep, muttering. The rear-view mirror showed her eyes still closed.

"Only to find out," I told myself, my son, and turned around, for the full view.

Her high-heeled shoes were basic and black, but looked well-preserved. She had on stockings, flesh-coloured, although they looked the same shade as her hands, so I didn't know what the point of that was. Her blouse was well-tucked into her skirt, although in her leaning position some of the fabric stretched tight over her torso, giving a snug fit for her breasts. I checked her neck – usually a pendant was a good giveaway, a cross or an Om or something. The Malays studiously avoided talismans, although I know that hadn't always been the case.

Her neck was bare.

The traffic was moving, and a car behind me honked. Bloody Cina feller, have big car means can keep horning taxi drivers. I drove forwards, and turned my windscreen wipers back on. We were in a valley of concrete, buildings on either side, with a dark sky shooting out jagged flashes of lightning. It reminded me of some of those English films that they brought to Rawang, the same kind of movies that I took people to see at KLCC, MidValley Mall, all the big time places. Maybe in that way KL was also now big time.

We were now on the main highway, and in a few turns I'd be in SS 2, but of course it didn't feel like that. A sign had gone up on the road, there were sirens, shouts, some lights. A police car stopped on the opposite side.

"Oh, finish, accident," I muttered to myself.

The slowing down this time would be more excruciating. I was still too far away to understand the nature of the accident, and getting closer would take much longer than I had expected.

I turned back to her. Her face was serene, as if she were a Bollywood heroine sleeping on a sunny field of flowers, and not in a dingy taxi in the KL monsoon. Her hair was cut to her shoulders, and didn't have the kind of straightness the Chinese girls' did. It was layered but not too thick, unlike my wife's, which fell to her knees in frizzy waves when she oiled it once a month, reminding me of the Malay banshee stories my grandmother used to tell.

I looked her over, again and again, for signs. I moved when the cars did, but I kept turning back. I was this close to figuring it out, I was sure of it, and when I did, I could triumphantly find something relevant to advise her on when she woke up. She would be pleasantly surprised, she would be impressed, she would think, what a knowing, intelligent man, he should not have been just an Indian taxi driver.

The accident was one car banging into another from behind because the front car had slowed down. Slippery roads, skidding possible, all kinds of things could have happened. I shook my head in disgust at the carelessness of KL drivers. What's the point of having big cars if you don't know how to drive properly?

Without meaning to, I turned around again, hoping she'd woken up. I could do with company again, however sour. But she was still slumbering, her ankles crossed demurely in front, her bag at the edge of the seat, almost jutting out.

Her bag.

Light brown, leather, looked branded, but probably

Petaling Street fake. Still, one look inside her purse and all will be well.

I made sure I checked the road and traffic conditions first. No accident for me, please, thank you. We were already in SS2, just a few minutes away, merely two more traffic lights. I slowed the taxi down so that the lights went red before I reached it. A Malay religious-type feller stopped behind me in a Mercedes E-class. Knowing I saw him in the mirror, he started gesturing and mouthing silent abuses. I only grinned back at him, and turned around.

Her bag had shifted even more forward when I braked, tempting me even more. This obviously needed to happen. It was out of my hands.

I undid the top zipper very slowly with my left hand, taking care not to make a sound. I checked the lights every ten seconds, and in about forty five seconds the bag was open. I put my hand in, feeling the contents. The lights changed. I drove slowly, keeping the steering wheel straight. The Imam overtook me, and I knew he wanted to catch my eye, but I wasn't going to give him the satisfaction.

I felt a phone, keys, a round thing that could be a compact, a long thing that could be lipstick, some papers, and then finally, just as the next light came up, a solid, comforting, bulging object, her purse, with the IC that will solve everything and let me have a good night's rest.

Since it was the heaviest thing in her bag, I lifted it gingerly, still keeping my eye on the lights. Two more checks, and I'll be in the safe zone. The purse was almost out. Light brown, matching the bag, same brand even, and maybe not even fake. I was impressed, and I was nearly there.

My phone beeped with my wife's text message.
Her eyes flew open.

As Kathi had expected, this time there were more boys at the clearing. He was the last arrival, puffing and panting his way towards them. Shafts of sunlight broke and shifted through the trees and fell on them, so that each boy had moving patches of grey over him.

Kathi noticed that Ah Liong stood a little apart from the others, his face blank, like the heroes of the comics they bought for two cents every week. Hanif and Bala were not looking at each other, and the others, Kok Leong and Azlan, boys who only came intermittently to the marble games, seemed to just want to watch some fun.

"So, you brought or not?" asked Hanif.

"Of course I did," said Kathi.

"We were all waiting for you, you know," said Azlan.

"I had to make sure all my marbles were with me, what," lied Kathi.

His scrambling around the house the night before, standing on chairs to reach keys and opening cabinets without any noise, was not something he was going to confess.

Everyone grew quiet, and Kathi eyed the rest, uncertain. It was time, but nobody seemed to want to declare it. The square object in Kathi's pocket, lodged between tiny balls of glass, seemed to grow heavy, and push downwards, wanting to drag Kathi onto the grass. He looked to his side at the pocket, and marvelled that he was still standing. The ground began to make waves.

Hanif cleared his throat. "Okay, come," he said. He stepped towards the middle of the clearing, to the spot where Kathi usually arranged his many-hued marbles.

Hanif put his hand in his pocket, and scanned the others around him, reminding Kathi of the koboi movies his father would take him to watch once or twice a year.

As if the rest thought the same thing, the other boys also took a step closer to Hanif. Kathi had to prise the previous cargo away from the mountain of marbles clogging his pockets.

"Nah, mine," said Hanif, taking the I.C. out.

"Mine," said Balan.

"There, mine," said Azlan.

"Nah," said Ah Liong, and Kok Leong followed suit. Kathi finally was able to get his package out, after three marbles of lavender, cobalt and crimson fell to the ground.

"There," he said.

All six cards were of the same size, that of their father's palms. They had photographs in the middle, and thumbprints on either side. There was an elaborate trellis design all over, intricate enough nearly to overtake the words written at the back.

The cards, gathered together that way, seemed like Kathi's marbles. Hanif and Afzal's were blue, Ah Liong and Kok Leong's were green. Kathi's was red.

"See! I told you!" said Hanif with triumph.

"What?" asked Kathi. He met Ah Liong's eyes.

"Eh, Hanif, don't start your bullshit again, lah," said Ah Liong. He turned to Kok Leong and began speaking in Cantonese. Kok Leong nodded, replied, then shrugged.

"Eh, what do you mean? And why you talking Chinese when we all here? Very rude you know!" said Hanif.

"You talk to Azlan in Malay, then, lah, I don't care," said Ah Liong.

"Why did you say I told you?" asked Kathi.

Hanif turned to him in momentary surprise, then smiled in a way that made Kathi want to hit him again.

"Wah, still haven't figured out, ah," he said. "Your cards all not blue, lah, not citizen."

Kathi checked his card again, and caught Kok Leong and Balan doing the same. Only Ah Liong remained unfazed, fixing Hanif with an aloof gaze.

"Your green, red cards all permanent resident only, not warganegara, you know. Only Azlan and me warganegara. You all pendatang!"

"Balan's is blue," said Ah Liong quietly. All eyes went to Balan, who seemed almost to wish his card was red instead. Under scrutiny, he presented his card again. The colour was like Kathi's mellow, dark blue marble.

"Eh, how come? You not Muslim, right, Balan?" said Hanif.

"My father born here," said Balan, and looked away. Kathi knew it was his eyes Balan didn't want to meet, and that he would no longer attend any marble games. Actually, Kathi wasn't even sure if there would be any marble games anymore.

"Yeah, but doesn't change the fact that you keling," said Hanif, and Kathi didn't know what he meant because he'd never heard the word "keling".

"Don't say that, you bloody naataan!" said Balan, and Kathi knew *that* word because his father said it to refer to people like Hanif.

"Ei, at least you blue I.C. lah, the rest here all komunis!" said Hanif. He looked at Azlan as he said it, and both boys broke into laughter.

"Komunis! Komunis! The gomen going to come and get you! Your father face there, komunis face!" said Hanif, but was on the ground before he finished his sentence, fighting for breath with Ah Liong on top of him. He yelped with pain as Ah Liong straddled him, and Kathi blinked, still not understanding what had happened. He heard the blows even though he didn't see them, and it was Balan rushing past who stirred him into action.

"Ei, enough, enough!"

"Okay, okay, everything okay."

Balan and Azlan held Ah Liong back. Hanif stood up slowly, in tears, blood flowing from his nose. Kathi heard a spitting sound come from Ah Liong. Hanif gave an enraged yell and fell on the Chinese boy.

Kathi watched without sound, without thought. If he had decided to move he would have done nothing more than fidget slightly. He would learn later, when it no longer made a difference, that Hanif was indeed making up stories; that he and his friends weren't communists. He would learn to recognise his father's sudden soft voice and unbreathing stance, such as when Hanif's father visited them later that evening, with a snivelling Hanif in tow.

He seemed to have received more blows. His face was tear-streaked, and his shirt had small splotches of blood from what seemed like caning. Amma held on to Kathi, with her hands on his shoulders.

"Eh, Ashok, I know boys will be boys, but what is this, man?"

"A schoolboy scuffle, that's all, Samad," said Appa.

"Still, you might need to discipline your son more."

"I did not hit Hanif," said Kathi, but Appa silenced him with a look.

"They had some idea of comparing I.C.s," said Appa. "We didn't even know he went off with it."

"It's only a card," said Hanif's father, and shrugged, a gesture that seemed both casual and merciful. Appa's face clouded over.

"Hanif said we're komunis," said Kathi, ending the sudden silence.

"Nonsense," said Kathi's father.

"Yes! Komunis! Pendatang! Keling!" burst out Hanif, through a film of snot and tears.

"Oh-woh!" Hanif's father shook his son playfully, as if chiding him for scoring a football goal at the wrong time. When he looked back at Appa, his face was smooth and diplomatic once more.

"These are uncertain times, Kathi, people are happy, but people are also scared, how we are all going to shape up. At such times, it's no benefit if we don't cooperate. We must all look out for each other, you see."

"I see, I see."

After Hanif and his father left, Appa sat down on the big chair next to the radio, as heavily as the day of the announcement. Amma made a cup of hot filter coffee, thick, frothy and steaming, and handed it to him. Appa didn't say a word.

"I'm sorry, Pa," said Kathi.

"Your son is apologising to you." Amma stated the obvious, but also went silent when Appa remained as he was. He sipped his coffee out of an aluminium davarah, his eyes on a spot on the cement floor. Kathi realised the I.C.-stealing had been a bigger thing than any other naughty pranks his father had scolded him for.

Appa finished his coffee and set the metal cup down firmly on the glass coffee table. The clink resounded around the house.

"What the hell does that naattaan think of himself?" he roared. "Think he can just walk in here and have his son call us names? Would they dare do it to the Chinaman? Ah? They think they so pure lah, bumiputera lah, what not. Ei, even that *word* is a Sanskrit word lah. What is so great about that, to be proud about when most of them can barely read or write? Think can compete with the Chinaman ah? Keling, my black arse! How you going to keep track of all the Seranis and Kristangs and Chindians, all the chinky-eyed Baba Muslims and Mamak beef-eaters, from one stupid card? You!" Appa suddenly leaned forward and pointed his finger at Kathi. "You better listen to this and not forget. You must study, understand? You must become big feller, show all the bloody Cantonese and Hokkien and Malay Muslim and all what not, that a Tamil feller will make it over the naattaan bastards. Sitting in their own country and doing nothing but scratching their crotches and bending over fives times a day, bloody stupid buggers. You stay with your own kind, you understand?"

Kathi would learn all this later, as he watched Ah Liong and Hanif fight and spit in the coconut grove, without yet such words forming in his head, coagulating and encrusting themselves, hard, solid, permanent. He could already see and understand everything from what was in front of him, and from his marbles, and their beautiful colours, the way they glinted separately in the sun, like jewels.

The Longan Seller

Kanmani came to the house an apparition, fully-formed. She spoke in a small, gentle voice and rounded out her *zhas*. Her husband and mother-in-law said she could wear anything. She showed up in cotton sarees with centre pleats folded neatly. They fell to the middle of her feet, a little after her toes. They fell that way every time.

Kanmani bought the groceries. She peeled and cut and cooked. She took her son to school and brought him back. She pressed her mother-in-law's feet in the afternoons. She supervised her son's homework. She knew if her husband had a bad day at work. She told her foreign maid she would find out immediately if she was being cheated.

The longan-seller came to the car when it was full of the family and Kanmani was sitting at the back by the window. He tapped on the glass during a red light and smiled at her. He had a grey scraggly beard and three missing teeth and his shirt was stained and torn. He scratched his armpit and raised his bunch of longans to the window. They were smooth and light brown, ripe and luscious. They just hung there.

"No, no, no," said Kanmani's husband. Her son came to the window and banged his fists on it. The longan-seller's eyes were on Kanmani.

Some nights later Kanmani walked out of the gates of the big house. She walked to the centre of town and found the longan-seller.

"My husband is proving to be a larger prick than the one he actually has," she said. He gave her a longan, picking it out of the bunch. She took it and went home.

Some nights later Kanmani walked out again and found the longan-seller. "My husband drives like a maniac, he shouts at other people when he cannot cope."

The longan-seller smiled and gave her another one.

Two nights later, Kanmani was back.

"My mother-in-law smiles all the time and then does not eat suddenly and my husband looks at me."

The next night, Kanmani said, "My son will not shit on his toilet unless I sit on the floor and cheer him."

She now had a lot of longans. She hid them in a bowl away from everyone. She sat down by the kitchen steps leading to the back of the house and looked at them. They looked back at her and smiled. She touched them. They had the softest fur on their skin, something she would not have noticed if she weren't looking so closely, if she had been thinking of something else. She bit into it. The skin was bitter. She spit it out. Inside the flesh was white. It was soft, translucent. Its juice ran out, down the skin, staining it darker. It ran down her fingers. Kanmani licked it. It was sweet, with a promise of tartness. She bit harder. The flesh obeyed. It came apart at her teeth's demand. It fell inside her mouth, it became masticated. They loved each other. They did it again and again.

And then she hit the hardness. It was hidden inside. She spat it out and it fell to the cement. It was very black, and solid like the stone she used to sharpen her knives. She took it and hit it against the ground. Nothing happened.

The next night Kanmani found the longan-seller. "My maid lies that she sees my mother's ghost in the house to get out of extra work," she said.

The longan-seller looked at her. His shirt was torn as before. He held his bunch of longans but did not move. Kanmani came back to the big house.

Kanmani ate all her longans, one by one. She collected the seeds and put them in a jar. She kept the jar by the stove so she could look at them as she cooked, and each time she glanced at them, she thought they looked more opaque, and became blacker, like obsidian. She thought they grinned back at her, every time their eyes met.

Kadaram

However much the car shuddered, my voice had to ring out. The words could not shudder like the car. "When you say it the way it is supposed to be said," Father had mentioned, again and again, ever since I had begun to read. "When you *really* say it, that's when there is actual meaning."

We were cloistered inside an Ambassador car on the dusty roads of Tamil Nadu, with the tour company driver slightly curious at the sight of us. Like our previous trips, this one was geared towards a destination concrete only in Father's vision. Sitting at the front passenger side, he dictated what I should read while I sat in the back seat next to my mother. He liked to dictate, to tell others what they should do with themselves. He liked knowledge, it gave him a rush, and he could forget himself for a little while and relish in mental connections. He would dictate that I get the same rush for myself, too.

This was an annual ritual, this trip to the Southern parts of India. It happened end of the year, during my school holidays, so that I could also participate. After the fourth year the process became comforting. We shopped for relatives. We packed communally in the living room. We made endless international phone calls, booking and cancelling travel agencies. We organised family meets.

We made lists of things to buy in Chennai. Our house in the small Malaysian town of Alor Setar would be a hub of chaos for about a week before departure, as we bundled ourselves to temporarily escape our reality.

My father's serious demeanour invariably transformed into unselfconscious excitement at the prospect of travelling in Tamil Nadu. The trips were usually his idea, and he decided the itinerary. It happened to involve family visits, but the real reason was to find old temples. The kind of temples built by kings of bygone dynasties, surviving as memorials to forgotten pasts. Father delighted in these structures with a childlike pleasure that was evident nowhere else. He knew their histories more than his own patients' and never tired of seeking more specimens, the quirkier the better.

This time, it was going to be an especially obscure town, named after its chief temple, Darasuram.

"What was it called initially?" he asked me, as I packed my own little suitcase, inserting tampons and pills for stomach cramps, away from his eyes. This was his test, to make sure I had read up enough.

"Rarasuram," I replied.

"Why?"

"Because that's from Rajarajasuram, which was the name of the town, named after Raja Raja Chola the second," I said, as if reciting my timetables.

"That's right! And it's the third out of?"

"Three, the other two being Brihadeeswara and Gangaikondacholapuram, the Great Living Chola Temples," I said. I sounded mechanical but he did not notice. All this had been drummed into me, over lunches, over drives, over eavesdropping on Father's conversations with his adult friends. He had spoken of the Tamil word for Kedah, the state we lived in. Only those residing in Malaysia would know of Kedah today, a northern state that bordered southern Thailand. We lived in its capital, Alor Setar. We gave this information out to new acquaintances in a slightly lower voice, as if hoping to skip past it, as if hoping they wouldn't have heard. An inconsequential town pretending to be a city in an inconsequential state so remote to foreigners that even the Lonely Planet had categorically printed that there was not much to see around here, despite being smack bang in the middle of Southeast Asia.

Kedah was Kadaram once, Father said. His friends had laughed. It sounded like a made-up word. Father had laughed along, but finished his story anyway. Yes, Kadaram. The Cholas of South India had conquered it, once. They had laid claim and ruled this land. His people. His ancestors. It had been a different kind of place, he seemed to want to prove.

The driver of our Ambassador glanced at his rear view mirror as I read out loud for my father. We were a slight oddity on the Tamil Nadu landscape. We spoke Tamil to the driver but we sounded different. We wore very modest Indian clothes but we walked like foreigners, he said, our steps too far apart, our arms dangling too freely. And more than anything, we gawked far more than deemed modest, even for out-of-towners. We reacted to the beggars, we covered our noses from bad smells, we delighted in street billboards of Tamil movies we watched in the privacy of our homes, we read Tamil signs out loud, as if it were a new language we had just come to understand. We were Tamil, he told us, and yet he had never seen Tamils like this before in his entire life.

"And you like all this?" he had asked father, as we

began our journey out of Chennai, gesturing out towards the muddied building facades and potholed streets.

"We come here every year for this," said my father, with a strange smile.

"Raja Raja Chola was also known as Arulmozhivarman." I recited out of Nilakanta Sastri's *The Cholas*, one of my father's historical bibles. The Ambassador lurched over a pothole, knocking out my mind. It punctured my sentence with a hiccough. "His son, Raja Raja Chola the second, built the Darasuram temple in the 12th Century AD. This temple is known as one of the Great Living Chola Temples, constructed between 10th and 12th Centuries. The legend with this temple is that the Shiva Linga was visited by Airavata, the divine elephant and steed of Lord Indra, king of the gods. The elephant bathed in the temple tank to lift a curse on itself, and hence the name of the temple deity, Airavateswara."

"Look at the years," said Father. He positioned himself in such a way that he was semi-turned to the back, always, towards mother and myself. "At that time, Europe was in the Dark Ages."

The road signs were in curvy Tamil script, simple enough for me to understand. Unlike other Indian-Malaysian children of my generation, I was not losing my native tongue, although I was nowhere near the literary sophistication of my parents, avid fans of classical Tamil literature. I derived my thrills from things like realising that Darasuram was less than 50 kilometres away. In Indian highway terms that meant another hour before we arrived.

"She must be hungry now," my mother noted, using my perceived discomfort to voice her own needs.

The driver veered off from traffic and braked on laterite dirt. We had packed a rudimentary lunch from our motel in the neighbouring village. *Idlis, sambhar,* chutney. Simple and typical. They had been hurriedly packed in banana leaves, folded over then wrapped in newspapers. Mushed up *idlis* ran with lentils and liquid. We ate them anyway, standing behind the Ambassador, baking in the arid heat. Our driver observed us with a certain detached intensity, as if on a zoo visit.

We only knew we had arrived in the town of Darasuram when our driver stopped at the temple. We had seen no welcome signs, no sudden surge of buildings or population. The landscape, with its paddy fields and sizzling heat, did not alter. Darasuram was a UNESCO World Heritage Site, but not a city stamped on the Tamil Nadu map. It was the smallest of the Chola temple triumvirate.

Peeking out from the car, I wondered if we had come to the right place. The structure was impressive, if not imposing, but it also seemed abandoned, as if left at a moment's notice. There was a handful of scattered tourists, some of them foreigners, like us, but mostly locals from other cities. An old man came out to greet us. He was hunched almost double, and if he weren't looking up at us he would probably have to stare at the floor the whole time. He was bare chested except for a string of cotton material slung across his torso, and he wore a soft cotton white *veshti* around his waist. He cried out a greeting so friendly we immediately warmed to him. He said he would show us around and speak in both English and Tamil, and that if we did not understand, we could ask him to repeat himself. He then smiled, turned around, and went back into the temple. We took it as our cue to follow.

He showed us feats in stone. A hundred pillars in the main hall, none of them alike in any sense. A bas relief of an elephant and a bull with a single conjoined head that made sense any which way you looked at it, like an optical illusion. A life-size statue of Goddess Saraswati tucked away in a dark corner wall, with detail so exquisite she had different sized fingernails. These were skills once considered normal, beautiful, and sacred, said the old man. The sculptures pointed to a past refinement, a sense of something having advanced upon itself, reaching a zenith before clambering down the inevitable mountain of civilisational decay.

We turned a corner, and instead of sculptures, there was writing on the granite wall. Father slowed his pace, letting the guide go ahead. We kept to his side. He scanned the words which were in grantha script, a precursor to the Tamil he knew.

"And there it is," he said, pointing at a particular spot on the wall. The old man paused ahead, then returned to us. He straightened his hunch a little to follow my father's finger.

"Kadaram," said the old man, and Father flinched as if the sound had touched his body. I peered closer at the spot. The word looked like a hieroglyph, and it sounded as strange as it looked. It stared back at me, the grooves smooth from expert chipping, the curves supine, put in place by a sculptor following an ancient decree. In that moment, it became that old, known place, the proof of the smoky arm of those before me, like me, who had reached out and explored, known, and claimed a foreign wonderland that I now saw as home.

I turned to Father. He was uncharacteristically silent. I must have imagined the glint in his eye. It was there one moment, and then gone. Perhaps it was the sun. I wondered if I said something now, really say it, it would make a difference.

The tour guide lowered himself back to his hunch and sighed. It made Father blink and look around, as if he had been in the same reverie.

"Kadaram is very far away," the guide said to my father.

"Not really. It's in Malaysia. We're from there."

The man shook his head. "Very far away."

He walked away.

Cake and Green M&Ms

I clutch the gifts tight to my chest, though I know they are not for me. I look around the strangely green universe of Brisbane that slides past my window like reels of film. The driver keeps asking Pa questions, and Pa answers. I keep eating my M&Ms with my free fingers, making sure I avoid the green ones. Those, I think, are just an awful mistake nobody took the trouble to correct. The reds, browns, even oranges, go with the chocolate taste, but green is just too different. I cannot make the greens belong in my head, even though I always see them in every packet.

After a while the taxi driver goes quiet, and so does Pa, and the world keeps throwing up green amidst the Tuesday traffic. Pa's big medical conference starts in Melbourne in a week, and Pa and I had saved up enough so we could arrive earlier to see his old friend in Brisbane. I had put all my pocket money into the piggy bank for six months to help Pa – all ten dollars of it. Pa was very proud.

"Shekar and I go a long way back, Kavita," says Pa.

"Yes, Pa."

"Since my university days."

"Yes, Pa."

"Have I told you how we met?"

"Yes, Pa." But I know I will hear it again, and I don't mind. Pa's stories are fascinating.

"It was my first semester at Monash, the first time I had left home, first time I had set foot in another country. And it was white-man country. Everything was new, different and very, very cold. I stayed in a really small dormitory, and one day when passing by this open door I heard Indian music coming from inside, and I thought I must be dreaming. So I had to stop, and listen to that music. I knocked on the door, and a few seconds later Shekar opened the door. I didn't like the look of him, but I could smell roast cardamoms. I knew I just had to get inside that room. So I introduced myself, and we've been fast friends ever since."

"Yes, Pa."

"We did everything together, just about everything. We went to lectures together, studied together, partied together, cheated together. We even tried to get each other dates on Saturday night, and..." Pa trails off, as he usually does around this point. I always want to ask him more, but never have the courage. Pa talks, I listen. That's how it has been since Ma left. I am happy with that equation. I clutch the gifts tighter and think of Leon, my teddy bear cramped inside the luggage in the boot.

When we get out at 371 Moggill Road Indooroopilly, I expect to see Uncle Shekar waiting for us at the gate, but there is no one. Maybe Uncle Shekar has mistaken our time of arrival – that would also explain why he wasn't at the airport. Whenever anyone from overseas visited Madras, Pa made sure the car was packed with as many family members as possible, to welcome the visitor with familiar faces. Pa says it is basic courtesy. Everyone knows guests are next to God and every wish and whim of theirs should be fulfilled.

Pa sets the bags down at the front door and presses a black button on the wall. I shift my weight, circling my arms tighter around the presents.

A boy of about seven opens the door. He looks at Pa, then me.

"Good evening, my young man, are your parents home?" says Pa.

The boy runs back into the house and we hear him yell, "Dad! Your friend from India is here!"

Uncle Shekar greets Pa with a quiet smile, and extends his hand. "Ratnam, it's such a pleasure."

Pa takes one look at Uncle Shekar, drops his bags and engulfs him in a bear hug. "Hello, Double S, look at you, it's been such a long time!" Pa's jelly belly wobbled into Uncle Shekar's thin wiry frame. I know sometimes it is hard to breathe like that and that is why Uncle Shekar disentangles himself.

"Yes it has, hasn't it? How long, exactly – ten years?" He helps Pa with the bags, and motions for the boy to go inside, but the boy stares at the gifts in my arms. The look on his face reminds me of my friend Anita when she accidentally swallowed her chewing gum – surprised and disgusted.

"Ten? Are you joking? More like twenty-five, Double S!" Pa says, trailing Uncle Shekar inside.

Uncle Shekar blinks, probably, I think, trying to arrange the years in his head. He takes us upstairs to the guest bedroom. "You just never notice the years passing, do you?" he says as he puts our bags down, struggling with the weight. "Well, Ratnam, hope you like the room. Mina will have dinner ready in about half an hour. She's at the shops at the moment. Bathroom's at the end of the corridor if you want to freshen up. And Kavita," he looks

110

at me for the first time, "you're taller than I thought. How old are you?"

Suddenly I cannot say anything, looking up at Uncle Shekar's soft brown eyes through his glasses.

"Go on, Kavi, he asked you a question," Pa says quietly.

"I'll be nine in June, Uncle Shekar," I say. He chuckles.

"Forget the "uncle", Shekar is fine," he says, standing straight. "I'm not that old, am I, Ratnam?" Uncle Shekar asks Pa.

I'm surprised. I cannot call anyone older than me just by their name. Ma had said it showed you didn't respect them. I look at Pa for guidance.

"You're always Double S to me, *yaar*," says Pa.

Uncle Shekar smiles but looks away. "My boy's Krishnan, Krish for short." He looks around for the boy, who's obviously not there, then shrugs. "Call me if you need anything, otherwise I'll see you in a while," he says, and leaves.

I look for Leon as I help Pa locate his towel and change of clothes. I notice everything in our room is covered with fabric – thick carpet, heavy curtains, floral wallpaper. There isn't a tile in sight, unlike our house in Madras. Yet everything seems as if it is meant to be there. Everything except our crumpled clothes and sweaty bodies. As Pa showers, I finally find Leon. I hug him hard and tell him not to worry.

We go downstairs for dinner, Pa in the shirt he'd set aside for the first day of the conference and me in my imported lace dress. I feel like one of the British colonials from Ma's stories, who dressed up in their jackets and bow-ties for dinner in the Indian summer. "Crazy idiots," Ma used to laugh.

I suddenly hear home-sounds coming from the kitchen – the clanging of metals and the emission of steam under pressure. It is strange to hear it here. I rush past Pa to the kitchen, and stop short. Aunty Mina is a tiny lady dressed like a teenager, in jeans, T-shirt and sneakers. When she greets us, her eyes fall on me first before travelling to Pa. They look warm and a little worried. Pa merely smiles, nods, says her name and joins Uncle Shekar in the living room.

Dinner is around a big glass table clear of any bric-a-brac. It seems too clean. It looks like they don't have to shove papers to one side to make room for meals, like I do at home. Aunty Mina brings out rice, lentils, steamed flavoured vegetables, a salad of lettuce and tomato, and some wine that Uncle Shekar opens to celebrate, but Pa lets me have only water. We eat so little I am not sure if this is just starters or actual dinner. I see Pa take second, even third helpings, and later, as they sit around talking, Pa occasionally spoons out the last bits of dal and vegetables onto his plate. I know he must still be hungry, but I don't know how to tell Aunty Mina.

Pa brings out the gifts after Aunty Mina puts the dishes away. He hands Aunty Mina the saree he and I had chosen carefully at *Nalli's*, wall tapestry for Uncle Shekar's office and a miniature cricket bat for Kris. Aunty Mina starts saying, "Oh, how beautiful, how lovely" even before I unwrap the gifts and does not stop for the next few minutes. The compliments come out automatically, like reciting a times table.

After the presents have been tested and stowed away, Aunty Mina serves us coffee, while Pa starts talking about his days in Monash with Uncle Shekar. I try to talk to Kris, but his English is so different I can barely understand him, and he keeps asking me to repeat my sentences, so I soon grow bored. Aunty Mina puts him to bed, and I occupy myself with newspapers, sitting at Pa's feet while he continues telling the stories I have heard so often – about trying to eat meat at the university canteen in his student days, because there was nothing vegetarian on the menu, and how he had vomited in the toilets later and missed two lectures, and –

"Ratnam, have you been to Mount Cootha?" Uncle Shekar suddenly asks.

"Excuse me?"

"Silly. Of course you haven't. Let's go now. The view of Brisbane from there is beautiful. Mina!"

And before we know it the four of us are packing into Uncle Shekar's car, which is almost as big as a bus.

"Can I bring Leon, Pa?" I ask. Pa looks down at me, blinks and frowns, as if he'd just remembered something. "I think Leon is afraid of heights, *ma*," he finally reasons, and gets in front with Uncle Shekar.

Pa is up by six o'clock the next day, very unlike him. When I come down to the kitchen a little hungry about seven, Pa is already at the breakfast table drinking coffee and eating toast with Uncle Shekar. He is asking after a lecturer at Monash, a Professor Caroline Stuart, whether Uncle Shekar knows if she is still there, and if he remembers how they used to make fun that she has two first names, and that the second sounded more appropriate. As Pa speaks with his mouth full, crumbs fly onto the table. I hadn't noticed it before, but in this house where I see Aunty Mina putting things back all the time like Ma used to, Pa's crumbs are obvious. Uncle Shekar does not say much, he listens and nods, drinking his coffee, though a couple of times I see him flick something away from the newspaper in front of him.

Kris is also at the table and he kicks my knees as soon as I sit down. I glare at him but he continues eating his breakfast, dressed in his school uniform.

"Would you like some toast, Kavita?" Aunty Mina asks, and places two buttered slices on my plate. "It's getting late, Shekar. And the kindy is a little out of your way."

"Surely Kris is still not in kindergarten?" Pa asks Uncle Shekar in surprise. The three of them laugh, but softly. "No, Ratnu, I teach there some days," Aunty Mina answers.

"Oh. So no one's going to be home?" Pa asks. There is a slight pause. I don't know what to do, so I take a bite of my toast. It tastes different, more starchy, and crumbs fall onto my plate. I want to wipe them away.

"I'll be home soon, old fellow," says Uncle Shekar. "I usually finish around four on Wednesdays. Nobody seems to like getting sick mid-week." He smiles but Pa doesn't respond. "Besides, today I absolutely must come home early, since we have that dinner to go to, right, Mina?"

Aunty Mina is fussing over me and Kris.

"Would you like some jam on that, dear? Kris, eat faster, you're holding us up."

"I am not!"

"I'm fine, thanks, Aunty Mina," I say.

"You're going out tonight?" Pa asks.

"No need to put the Aunty in front, dear. Just Mina will do."

"Sorry, Ratnam, we were invited over a month ago, and we cannot cancel this. It's a friend's engagement – "

"But I haven't seen you for – "

"Shekar." Aunty Mina's voice stops everyone but Kris, who suddenly thinks it's a good idea to finish his cereal

114

quickly like his mother told him to. "I'm sorry, but we're really going to be late."

"Yes, dear."

I help Aunty Mina clear the table. She puts all the plates and forks and knives into something like a washing-machine under the kitchen sink, and I hear water sounds after she presses a button. She tells me it's a dishwasher.

Again, like last night, the family is out of the house and in the car within minutes. I watch from the front door as the car pulls away, and I see Aunty Mina waving at me. Somehow I know everyone will get to their individual destinations in time, and that is the way things happen. That must be how everyone does it here. I don't wave back.

I close the door and go back to the kitchen. It's very quiet and I want to make some noise, but I am not sure what kind as I am usually quiet, like when in a class without a teacher or when I don't want to talk to other children at Pa's parties.

I play with Leon all morning, and Pa lets him sit with us during lunch, which doesn't happen very often. I eat as little of yesterday's leftovers as possible, partly because it is too bland, and partly because I know Pa needs more.

"Do you think they'd have any chilli sauce?" Pa asks as I coax Leon to eat. I instantly understand and search the fridge and pantry until I find an opened bottle of Maggi Mild Chilli Sauce. It has some effect on the food. The bottle is half-empty by the time we're finished. I place it far inside the pantry as I clear up.

Pa takes his post-lunch nap on the couch, and I go upstairs to explore. First is the small bedroom with a single bed. The covers are dark blue, and have cartoon drawings of a yellow-coloured boy with large round eyes and jagged-edged head. The words "Bart Simpson" are written all over. I hop onto the bed and look around. The room is filled with posters of cartoons and sportsmen. I see a basketball in a corner, and next to it, a cricket bat and ball and bales. All real, none mini-sized.

I get off and enter the biggest room. The bed is the biggest I've ever seen, and there's a door leading into a bathroom. I realise this is the best bedroom in the house, and Uncle Shekar and Aunty Mina must sleep here. I wonder why they hadn't given their bedroom to Pa and me, like how Pa would give up his room to anyone staying with us. Maybe they thought the bed would be too big for just one man and a child.

I go to their dressing table mirror, but can only see myself up to my chest. There are many bottles with words I don't know yet on them, and flat squares in many colours. I pick up a framed photograph of Uncle Shekar, Aunty Mina and a baby. I know that must be Kris. He isn't a cute baby, and I frown. I realise my thinking that babies must be cute is wrong. They look like they are on a beach. Aunty Mina is wearing a straw hat, and Kris and Uncle Shekar have identical pink plastic flower garlands. I recognise the Australian flag in Aunty Mina's hands, because Pa told me about it on the plane. They're all squinting and smiling at the camera.

"Kavita!"

I nearly drop the photo in fright. I put it back exactly where it was and run downstairs to answer Pa.

A white lady drops Kris off later in the evening when it is dark, and says we don't have to worry about his dinner. We watch television together as Pa and I eat another round of leftovers with chilli sauce. Kris is monosyllabic to Pa's polite questions, and tries to pull my ears when Pa isn't looking. I push him away.

"Don't, idiot, it's painful," I whisper to him.

"Of course it is, that's why I did it," he hisses back.

"You are so childish," I say, in exactly the same way I've heard Ma telling Pa.

"What?"

"I said – You. Are. So. Chil. Dish. Do. You. Un. Der. Stand?"

"You talk like a retard."

I don't know what "retard" means. "You have Bart Simpson blankets."

"What?"

"Bart. Simp. Son. Blank. Ets."

"So?"

"So, all childish people have Bart Simpson blankets. Everyone knows that."

Kris gapes for a few seconds, gauging the grain of truth in the statement. At that moment both Uncle Shekar and Aunty Mina arrive from their dinner party, and attention is diverted.

"Look what we brought," says Aunty Mina, holding a white cardboard box. I already know what it must be. Whether in Madras or Brisbane, cake boxes seemed the same.

"What is it? What is it?" asks Kris. I only raise my eyebrows. Pa looks up from the television at Uncle Shekar, who is smiling.

"Chocolate Mud Cake, Ratnam. Remember?"

I remember. Both Pa and Uncle Shekar were going to sit for their Air-nuh-toh-mee exam the next day, and decided they needed a break and took a walk, which led them to a café. Convinced they had earned a treat, they decided to share a slice of cake, and picked the darkest chocolate cake they could find. They had nearly finished it when Pa had asked a passing waitress the name of the cake. When she said it was Mud Cake Pa had nearly thrown up again. "In this weird country you never know what they put in their food," he had complained, and it had taken the manager half an hour to convince him there was nothing remotely muddy about Pa's cake. "So much for Anatomy," Pa had told me.

Pa laughs. "Yes, Double S, I do remember."

Aunty Mina cuts the cake in the kitchen, while Kris takes out some plates and forks. Pa leads me to the kitchen and we both watch as the cake is neatly sliced. I can almost smell the chocolate.

"It looks delicious, Mina," Pa says, and I know he means every word, because he looks into Aunty Mina's eyes. Pa wipes his hands on a dry cloth, picks up two of the pieces and hands me one. Something is right about this but something is also wrong. Aunty Mina remains silent as Pa leaves for the living room. I follow, taking my first bite.

"Oh, for God's sakes, Ratnam, can't you use a plate?"

I freeze, the pieces in my mouth heavy as a stone. I know it is Uncle Shekar's voice, but it doesn't sound like him at all.

"Doesn't matter, you can eat it like that, Ratnam," Aunty Mina says, very quickly. I look at her eyes, and they are not looking at Pa.

Pa comes back into the kitchen slowly. Kris puts plates and forks with napkins on the dining table, and Pa places his slice on one of them. I follow his example, and suddenly feel Pa and I are like the green M&Ms. I want to cry.

Later the cake is nearly finished, and Pa has been silent for a while. Suddenly he says, "I think I might catch an earlier flight to the conference, Shekar."

"Really?"

"Yes, it's probably best to be well-prepared, I think. I mean, I know it doesn't really start till Saturday, but I just thought it might be good to settle in earlier. I might take Kavita to Monash grounds, show her around a little. Right, *ma*?" Pa smiles down at me. I look up at him but don't answer.

"Ratnam, look, I know we haven't really been around – "

"Oh, don't be silly – "

"But it is the middle of the week and we're busy and – "

"Of course, of course."

"We're just – "

"I want to see Monash," I say suddenly, without knowing why. Everyone goes quiet, and Pa looks at me with a slight smile.

"That settles it, then."

The next morning both Pa and I are up, bright and early, for the 7.05am flight to Melbourne. Uncle Shekar has offered to drop us at the airport, but Pa said we will take a taxi. Both Pa and I bustle around packing everything, and this time I make sure Leon is not stowed away somewhere. Pa seems a little hurried, so I don't want to disturb him, but I ask him to zip up my blouse as it was at the back. He turns me around, and I see our reflections in the mirror in front of me.

"Are you going to miss Uncle Shekar, Pa?" I ask as he struggles with the zip.

"Yes, of course."

"Really?"

Pa looks up at my reflection, then gets back to the zip.

His face seems a little different now, as if he'd blown a balloon really big only to have it burst.

Breakfast is fast and quiet, and Uncle Shekar calls for a taxi afterwards. Once it arrives, he helps Pa load the luggage. Aunty Mina hugs me, and thanks Pa for the gifts. Kris does not say much, except a small "bye" just as we're about to leave. I say "bye" too as I get in the back, and watch as Pa and Uncle Shekar shake hands and say they'll be in touch.

Once Pa gets in the taxi, the driver pulls away, and Pa and I wave to the three of them standing on their front lawn. Pa pulls down his window and says, "We'll meet soon, Double S!" and laughs. They disappear from view.

"Why do you call him that, Pa?"

Pa rolls up the window, and pauses for a second. "It stands for Sweaty Shekar."

"Sweaty Shekar?"

"Yes, he was Sweaty Shekar. Double S. Couldn't say a word, always nervous, always sweating when he talks. Especially to girls. The beads of sweat would roll down his forehead as if he'd just run a marathon. He was very bad with the girls. I always had to step in and rescue him. Always found him a date on Saturday nights. For which he was very grateful. Always."

"Oh." I want to ask Pa about sweat and marathons and dates, but his story isn't over, and I want to hear it out because I haven't heard this one before.

"Even at his wedding he was scared, the poor guy. He had begged me to come earlier than the other guests. I had to calm him down, told him arranged marriages weren't that bad. Told him it was the best thing to have ever happened to him," Pa pauses again. "And I think I was right."

"Really? Why?"

"Because now he is a family man, Kavita. And it suits him. Don't you think it suits him?"

I don't answer, because I don't know. I only look out the window, holding Leon, and wonder if Melbourne will be as green as this.

The Last Day of a Divine Coconut

It is time for me to say goodbye. I am on my way to getting cracked to smithereens at temple. Someone has already bought me, presumably some rich Chetty wanting to fulfill a vow of breaking 108 coconuts because his boy scored straight As in school recently. That's usually the deal. I am in my semi-naked state, stripped of my shiny green soft cover, but am allowed to retain my brown inner hardness. I have passed through at least three hands already, from Adivel to Kumar to Murugan now. Murugan carries me with my siblings on top of his head, and I am parked on a huge silver vessel by the side of the Kandaswamy temple steps this morning. The sun pretends to rise and shine on the smog of Brickfields, Kuala Lumpur, just as all of us here pretend we're not in Kuala Lumpur, Malaysia but Madras, India.

Pretty soon the streets will become searingly hot, and pedestrians out to buy their spices and incense will also find an excuse to step into the air-conditioned shops for some rice and curry on banana leaves. And me, I will have to await my fate here, both dreading and welcoming the moment of my demise. I welcome it because this is why I have been created, this is my purpose (so they tell me) in life, my ultimate fulfilment – to make a man feel pious. I dread it because I do not yet know what I will be in my next life. Do I merit being born an animal? A goat maybe, waiting to be sacrificed on Hari Raya Aidiladha, the day of the Muslim sacrifice. Or perhaps I will regress into being a pandanus plant, worthy only of flavouring a breakfast nasi lemak. In any case, times like this give you pause. I look back on this life, spread out the tentacles of my awareness, and wonder if I have done comparatively well.

You see, I'm one coconut out of millions around the world that get sacrificed on temple altars for the ego of my buyers. I'm a part of a Hindu ritual, a specifically South Indian ritual, that symbolises the perishing of the human ego, the Id, on the altar of the eternal, a necessary step towards spiritual enlightenment. This is supposedly the goal of every self-respecting Hindu everywhere in the world.

And how many Hindus there are in this world! If my fellow coconuts are to be believed, the numbers are in dispute, ranging from 800 to 1120 million. And this isn't counting all the Indians who are Muslims, Christians, Zoroastrians, who don't mind ducking into a Hindu temple every now and then, just to be on the safe side. And yeah, sure, I have some cool coconuts who're in India itself, smugly waiting on their trees to be plucked and delivered within the local village, but the real deal are those comrades who get shipped out to places like this one, these little pockets of pretend India within the most non-Indian spots on the globe. Southall in London. Jackson Heights in New York. Gerard India Bazaar in Toronto. Tsim Sha Tsui in Hong Kong. Dandenong in Melbourne. We don't get to decide where we're headed, but sure, none of us complain about it. It means a more prolonged wait for the final throw, and you get to travel a bit, see the sights along the way. And then there are the more localised Little Indias around here, the ones that have enough trees of their own to supply the temples. Paco in Manila, Mogul Street in Rangoon, Pasar Baru in Jakarta, Phahurat in Bangkok. Serangoon Road in Singapore. Can't escape the Indians, they're everywhere – one in every fourth person on the planet now. Then there's me and my close brothers in Brickfields, Kuala Lumpur. We're the cheaper ones, you know. We don't have import costs slapped on our copras.

There is a part of me that wishes I had been thrown into a different box on the Honda lorry, one that would have taken a trip straight to an aircraft carrier, rather than to a local inner city ethnic spot. And this is a bit of a sorrowful thing, too – somehow, being a Malaysian coconut seems slightly insignificant compared to being a diasporic Indian coconut of the United States. Coconuts from here that have reached there have been asked if Malaysia is situated in Africa. Sad but true. Still, it would've been interesting to see how they live, those who come over here for their holidays and stare wide-eyed at everything. I would like to get a little wide-eyed too, however temporarily.

Anyhow, I take comfort in the fact that we coconuts are constantly in demand, to fulfil the global Hindu's attempt at cosmic redemption. And this is a different thing to being opened and cut out and squeezed and boiled and crushed for things like milk and oil and fuel and roofs. I am now thankfully not so mundane. No, this selection to be sacrificed is a special thing. It makes us, until the moment of our death, something akin to divinity. I am holy till I die. I don't mind being divine. It beats being in a curry. I will admit that I will sort of miss this existence though. See, I've already whispered this to the others crowding around me in this vessel, and we all tend to agree. Despite not being as famous as my Western cousins, there's something about having been picked for sacrifice in a Little India. It makes me feel a bit special, the fact that my impending end is part of a ritual in a place that, if left to natural history, would not exist. It's like dying inside a dream, although the event itself is real enough. The fragility of such a concept.

Now I'm not very popular when I start saying these things, especially with the brothers who're about to get onto cargo planes out to China and England. But the fact remains that these cultural enclaves came into being because humans migrated to a foreign place, and end up placing walls between themselves and strangeness. Whether they were successful at it, though, is another matter altogether.

You see, I think this web of mini-Indias mushrooming around the world is both artifice and a necessity. Like the sister phenomenon of Chinatowns everywhere, these Little Indias recreate the Indian motherland within its small vicinity. A little ambitious, considering you're theoretically trying to cram the equivalent of 22 languages, 28 states, at least 33 separate cuisines, and 12 known ways to wear the sari, into the length and breadth of a single street or suburb. The result is usually a diluted mish-mash of food and clothes and shops and temples. These may seem faintly recognisable to a visitor from India, but if locals who've only known Little India all their lives were to pay the mothership itself a visit, they would quickly figure out what had been "Indian" to them are actually semi-shadows of the real thing. And that's what these enclaves are, really, at the end of the day. Shadows of another culture that remain like a mirage despite all the painstaking efforts to plant them.

So you see, I'm divine not just because I've been marked to be offered to the gods, but because I am both real and unreal. This role I now have to perform, this suicide I am looking forward to and share in spirit with my global brethren, is merely the result of historical accident. It is very easy to wonder what might have been, what this area we call Brickfields would have turned out to be, had the British not gotten it into their heads, at some point during the Industrial Revolution, to go out and save the rest of mankind. I'll try to be brief about this, because really, while I sit here on the basket with my friends, I don't really know how much time I have before I am air-lifted by human hands into the *sanctum sanctorum*. See, for all the talk of this place as a Little India, it was actually developed by a Chinese man, Yap Kwan Seng, the 5th and last Kapitan of Kuala Lumpur, around 1890. The Kapitans were Chinese repress-entatives of their own enclaves who had to report to the British on local whispers and events. He came to Malaya from Chak Kai district in China and quickly realised Kuala Lumpur was expanding, and that people were looking to settle there. A fire in 1881 that razed wooden houses to the ground had prompted a British by-law requiring all houses to be built only with bricks. So Yap Kwan Seng constructed a kiln, baking bricks from the clay all around this place. Good clay, apparently, which made good bricks, making the place famous. So it's possible some smart young British officer decided to name this spot Brickfields. It has a ring to it, doesn't it? A hundred and fifty years later, the official name of the street is now Jalan Tun Sambanthan, named after an Indian politician who helped negotiate Malaysian independence in the 1950s. But still, any self-respecting taxi driver is more likely to take you on as a customer if you say "Brickfields".

Now, the British also took their railways seriously. As they had done in India, they developed a railway system for Malaya, and decided to place the main depot of Malayan Railways in Brickfields. And this is where it starts. It was easier to import those from another colony, who already knew how to work the railway systems there, rather than having to train the local natives from scratch. So they brought droves of Indians into Malaya. They brought them in from Madras State, the closest colony to Malaya, having the shortest turnaround time by ship. The Tamil-speaking Indians naturally settled into prepared quarters around the Brickfields depot. They opened schools, worked in administration, and, like today, went to temple and broke coconuts.

I must stress here, though, that because of the way Brickfields formed itself, it is both sibling to the Southalls and Jackson Heights of the world, and yet it isn't. See, unlike those places, which established themselves as a result of voluntary migration, the Little Indias around here, in Southeast Asia, are the result of colonial policy. As such, there was never any insistence or debate that the Indians assimilate themselves into the local society. The British preferred it if they kept to themselves – in fact they even encouraged it, in keeping with the "divide and rule" policy. Time passed, more Indians came in, and the next generation of Indians born in Malaya began to grow and marry and have children themselves. Thrust far away from home and not being told what the new place was like, the Tamils erected a fortress of familiarity all around them, never needing to leave. Brickfields grew in terms of infrastructure and administration. More shops opened, and the 100 railway quarters of Rozario Street were filled to the brim. More temples were built, because why have one when you can have several? So there's the Buddhist Maha Vihara, built by Theravada Buddhist Sri Lankans but frequented today by the Chinese, the Zion Lutheran Church, the Church of Our Lady of Fatima, a Karpaga Vinayagar Temple, and a mosque called Madrasatul Gouthiyyah. All places of worship designed for those of Indian origin. All still stand today, ancient architecture intact, giving Brickfields the moniker "Divine Location". The term is now in all those Lonely Planet books, bringing in lots of foreign visitors, who stand around trying to emulate the rituals but also looking a little lost. Fair enough, they're here for an unbroken antiquity they have not experienced. Even this temple I'm in, the Kandaswamy temple, is easily a hundred years old. More evidence justifying my current holiness. As time has passed, though, Brickfields has become more an inherent characteristic of Kuala Lumpur than a divergent feature, connected to India in spirit and to Malaysia in commerce.

Now I have heard back from some of the other coconuts around the world before they went on their own last pilgrimage towards sacrifice, and it sounds like these nests of India in the West are different in a regional sense as well. Many of the Indians in the US and UK are of the North – and that's like a whole other country, you see. The language, the cuisine, even the marital rites, bear no resemblance to anything that the Southern Tamils could recognise. Tamils are rice-eaters, while the Punjabis and Gujaratis of the North prefer rotis. Southerners wear the saree differently, follow a different caste-system, even build their temple deities using different stone materials. So if an outsider took it into his head to visit all the Little Indias of the world, expecting them to be more or less the same, he would be in for a shock. These regional differences may have been buried under the umbrella of a more hegemonic "India" within the country itself, but would jump out in a concentrated form in foreign locales to the random observer. So no single Little India in the world is wholly the same, culturally and even linguistically. And of course, thanks now to Bollywood, the biggest Indian export since Mahatma Gandhi inspired Martin Luther King, everyone thinks Indians speak Hindi, and only Sri Lankans speak Tamil, and therefore don't really register a South Indian Little India on any diasporic map – especially one in an Asian country.

And yet here I am, waiting for the prayers to start, in the full knowledge of other coconuts having been broken before and after me, in places ranging from ten to a thousand miles away. I imagine myself connected to all those other coconuts in some Rushdiesque way, a web of interconnecting lines between me and my siblings trespassing across man-made lines on maps. What if, by some strange circumstance, all the Little India temples of the world each broke a coconut simultaneously? What a collective crack that would be – one global gunshot.

Aiyoh! That was close. It was just the priest passing by, getting his instruments ready for the afternoon prayers. I'd thought the Chetty had come. It's usually the whole family, really, clamouring away. And everything then happens so briskly, with all the bells ringing, the incense and camphor smells in the air, the priest chanting in Sanskrit as he throws flower offerings to the Lord Murugan in the main altar, and then boom, time for the coconut breaking in the special concrete tub by the side. But no, I think I have some minutes left, to ponder the little absurdities of the universe. You know, what if, for instance, I happened to roll off this basket, roll my way out of the temple, out onto Scott Road? Yes, I admit I'm probably having some jitters about my last day, but that is probably reason enough for me to indulge in this temporary fantasy of freedom, right? So yes, if I were rolling around Scott Road and then went along Jalan Tun Sambanthan before turning off into Jalan Rosario, I could perhaps say a last goodbye. Like to the air-conditioned restaurant that serves meals on torn banana leaves, and smells of roasted cardamom. Or the row of textile shops, with chiffon and georgette sarees hung-up fanlike from the ceiling, as Tamil film songs blare from speakers larger than the salespeople within. And especially those little makeshift stalls that crop up around Hindu temples, selling garlands of jasmine and rose and marigold. They're in my family, too, being accessories to prayer.

But then if I were to roll a bit further away, out of this area, what would meet my eye is not the clean contrast between colourful Indian ghetto and the organised streamline of polished urbanity, but just more hodge-podge chaos. I would see the incredibly tall Petronas Twin Towers, evacuated right after 9/11 as a safety measure because some high official overreacted to its global importance. I would see KL Sentral, the railway station that has replaced the Malayan Railway depot, and is now the focal point of all five inner-city railway lines. But you know, this stuff is just the surface, obscuring all the other things that are still somehow there, breathing and surviving in this polluted air. Underneath this sheen is the chaotic tumble of the real Kuala Lumpur, the one that has always defined its growth, pre- or post-independence. That illegal book-seller, for example, who prints his own edition of the current bestsellers and sells them from a wooden cart with iron wheels as high as his waist. You never know his name, and you never know where he's going to appear next, and you know enough not to ask. You just hope to get lucky one day and find him around your street corner. The Coliseum Theatre, built in Art-Deco style in 1920 by the Chua family, shows Tamil movies to this day. There's a woman who works under the awning of that building, selling homemade fried snacks stuffed into little plastic packets. She wears a batik sarong every day because it helps with the heat, and she's sent her son to study medicine at Oxford with her profits. And then there're the ubiquitous Eun Yan Sang shops scattered around the place, selling traditional Chinese medicine, famous enough to warrant Indian and Malay regulars.

I could perhaps make a quick getaway from here, except that taxi drivers agree or disagree on whether or not they take a passenger, depending on the passenger's requested destination and the possible state of traffic leading there. Most times, if they do agree, it's on a set price that has nothing to do with the meter. Trying to haggle is useless. And if by chance we get caught for speeding, I can always gently query, "Lima puluh?" to the police officer, and be let off for a mere fifty ringgit. Traffic slows down for everything, but especially so if there's been an accident on the other side of the road, because everyone notes down the vehicle's registration numbers to use on the next lottery ticket. Traffic also slows down every time it rains, which is usually on a daily basis, and usually between 3:30 and 4pm, like clockwork. And oddly enough, it doesn't wane on Friday afternoons, when the rest of the city stops its business for the holy Muslim prayers.

The three eyes I have would see all this, and I must confess, sometimes I wonder why Brickfields needs to be called "Little India" in the first place, when it is not that starkly distinguishable from its surroundings. Its chaos is also the chaos of Kuala Lumpur, its fragmented existence also an aspect of the Malaysian way of life. In fact, much of the Malays' mode of interfacing with the world, in terms of language, culture and food, comes from pre-Islamic Indian influences, from the Hindu-Buddhist empire of Srivijaya and Majapahit, when Sanskrit was the *lingua franca* and temples to Vishnu and Shiva were prominent. The residue of that history is visible not just in Malay words that have come from Sanskrit, like *manusia* and *dewa* and *raja*, for "man", "god", and "king", or in the shadow puppetry that re-tells the Hindu epics of the Ramayana and Mahabharatha, but also in the way both the Malays and Indians today practise social courtesy. It's in the little things, like asking permission before crossing in front of seated elders, in bringing fruit when visiting the sick, and in the *bersanding* wedding ritual, in which the bride and groom sit beside each other as the rest of the family blesses them in turn.

Moreover, after independence in 1957, the first Prime Minister, Tunku Abdul Rahman, declared all Indians and Chinese in Malaya were citizens of the new independent nation, no questions asked. Fifty years later, you would think this means the average Indian is as much a local as his Malay neighbour. That just as Indians are spread around the Malay land, mixing in with the current milieu, so too would their collective identities merge and mesh with the local environment.

But somehow, despite being here in Little India,

witnessing so much business and trade among Indians, I also sense their collective presence in another aspect. Brickfields here is the home of Ananda Krishnan, one of the richest men in Asia, who owns Maxis, the mobile network, as well as Astro, the satellite television company. Yet he, the rich Indian, is the rare exception. He is the one that the majority of Indian – the toilet cleaners, bus drivers, mechanics, waiters, factory workers, office clerks, and checkout girls of the nation – speak about in hushed tones. They say his name with reverence, because they know he made it against government-sanctioned odds, living the life the rest of them don't even dare dream of. Especially not when, fifty years on, they still hear Malays telling them to go back to where they came from.

Maybe that's why not many shop owners along Brickfields like the new developments that happened last year. You can't fool them. The rally of 2007 still hangs like a spectre, when thousands of Indians took to the streets demanding 4 trillion US dollars from the Queen of England as compensation for the colonial practice of assisted migration. Barisan Nasional, the Malaysian ruling party, knows it has to be a little careful, after being publicly exposed for neglecting its minorities, especially after a White House rebuke. So when the Indian Prime Minister, Manmohan Singh, planned to pay a visit in November 2010, things went into overdrive from August of that year itself. It was all over the papers. Refurbishment for Brickfields. Little India to be updated. A 35 million ringgit project to "spruce up" the place, planned so well it had three phases to get through. They made Jalan Tun Sambanthan a one-way street. They posted countless policemen there to fine illegally parked vehicles, day and night, without providing alternative parking spaces. This, despite such parking being part of the driving norm of the city. They widened the roads, then constructed ornate arches and Indian-style street lights all along them. They created the tallest fountain in the country, with elephant motifs. There was even a post-modern, larger-than-life street sculpture of Nataraja, Shiva as the lord of dance, rendered in solid cubist style. The Indian Prime Minister came, stood on a raised platform and gave a gentle speech, as did many other dignitaries. The public later thronged the streets for late night concerts with specially flown-in Tamil film celebrities. Random Indians were interviewed by Vaanavil, the local Indian satellite channel, extolling the virtues of the "new" and "developed" Brickfields, and how it was so different now compared to "the olden days", so much better.

But none of this is enough to cover the consequence of such cosmetic developments. I should know – I hung on my tree for months, getting fatter and fatter, waiting to be plucked before I became overripe and fell down useless to the ground. Business throughout Brickfields suffered, for eight whole months, while construction happened. The one-way street drastically reduced lunchtime customers in the restaurants, who in turn needed less coconut milk because there was a surfeit of curries. People went to other saree stories, other grocery shops, other temples. I felt so out of the loop, I was even willing to settle for being converted into fuel, to be used by illegal refugees and prostitutes living between the cracks of Brickfields, too scared officially to buy gas for their stoves. You would think the authorities would have had the basic sense to sort out the parking and traffic situation before starting construction. And you would wonder at the necessity of this refurbishment, so pleasing to the eye. I don't know how it helps the temple owner, the garland seller, the little boy looking after the tourists' shoes as they enter these temples to take a million pictures and gawk at the sacrosanct. Obviously, it didn't help me.

Now when you look around the area, it is so pretty you wouldn't have a clue it was the spot that provided bricks for the rest of the city at one time. There's even a gaudy arch on the far end of Jalan Tun Sambanthan, with welcome greetings in Malay and Tamil, announcing loud and clear where you are. The streets have floral patterns in coloured cement, branding the area, drawing clear boundaries on area and identity. It looks like the government finally did what those in Brickfields had been trying to do for themselves for many years. The effect, though, is slightly stifling, like a label slapped across a mouth. Perhaps it's supposed to make it even harder for those within Brickfields to leak out, or allow others to leak in. It's very clear now where the Indians belong, now that they've been put in their place. Sometimes it's as if the British never left.

Except that these things also scream about where and what Brickfields is, and they're useful for those who don't know of its existence, like the tourists from the other side of the world. They come through Kuala Lumpur for a few days, laying over before jetting off to Singapore or Thailand or Indonesia. Naturally the other places are more interesting, but they come here anyway so they can later say they've done *all* of Southeast Asia, including Malaysia. They come to Brickfields for the exotic, and they stay for the – well, I don't know, really, I don't see that they want to. They take in the sights and sounds of Little India for about half a day. They buy brass figurines, eat spicy food with their hands, tape the

Tamil music on their iPhones, and feel the marvel and wonder they are here to seek. They are, I've been told, the real reason for the sudden decision on decoration – they inject money into people's veins. And I think it's worked, because they crowd in almost on a daily basis now, smiling at everyone around them. And why wouldn't they? I've seen reticent street pedlars call out to them, quiet women smile up at them, taxi drivers slowing down for them. The Japanese and Chinese tourists don't receive this treatment – only the British and American and Australian ones. Some of the older coconuts, plucked too late to be of any use and chucked by the wayside, say there are many reasons for this – because they look like people on television, because they look so odd on Jalan Tun Sambanthan, because they remind the locals of a time when people like them owned everything, because they remind the locals that they still own everything.

I hear the temple bells ringing. There they are, the hordes of devotees walking in. They are in their best, coloured silks. The men stand to one side of the altar and the women on the other. They bring their palms together to salute divinity as the Brahmin priest drones on. I know enough not to be taken in by the seeming piousness – this is really a fashion show for the ladies, and a pick-up point for the men. There, it's started already – a few of the younger ones, whose palms face the Lord but the eyes are to the right, checking out the row of ladies. Once the prayers are over there would be more eyeing of each other going on, and if the girl's parents aren't looking, perhaps a smile.

But I will not know what happens next. This is the drawback to being divine. It is limited to lifespan. And I have been chosen, anointed even, to expire early, rather than rot on some random field. It's okay, I tell my brothers who're crouched around me, it will be over soon, swift and sudden, and besides, I will depart having made an impact, and hopefully on many levels. I will give out that great satisfying smash, heard by all in the street like a gunshot from a Hollywood movie. I will have fulfilled the emblematic Hindu act, existing since millennia ago. And I will then find out if the whole thing about the divine is true, if I have truly, even if fleetingly, symbolised something as profound as the destruction of human ego.

Oh, I hear it now, low voices, money exchanging hands. My compatriots quiver – I refuse to join them. I only wish I could close my three eyes, so I wouldn't have to watch the ground zoom up at me. Some of the brothers are being picked up. The bells ring louder, the chanting is endless, I feel the wind whoosh at my tendrils. Moment of truth, ladies and gentlemen. It's been a good life, and at least it's been at a place where, despite some issues, cultures have been mixed-up together for so long, that I actually don't feel bad at not having left, at not having seen things. All foreign things are already here, all have already been localised, so that I feel I've already seen it all, even if in miniature, in this mongrel place. I wish it will go on as it is even if I cease to be, and perhaps my temporary divinity will ensure a longer and different life in the next birth.

Here it comes. The hands are firm, strong, but also seem tentative, like they aren't sure what to do with me. Some fingers prod my hard shell, and they're surprisingly soft, without the calluses I've been told about. Nevertheless, I am lifted up, and all of a sudden I see the vista of Kuala Lumpur, its roads and traffic and buildings and people, all in flux. The fingers fumble around, and partially obscure my eyes. I try to squint as I'm hurtled to the ground. I can't be certain, with this partial sight, but it very much seems like the hands holding me were white.

Circular Feed

Yes, that's him, said Zya to Khalid, he said he was going to do it, and now he is. That's brave of him, Khalid told Yusuf later at dinner, but Yusuf only shook his head, brave and stupid are different sides of the same coin, he said, he was going to get himself killed. That's a bad attitude, said Khan, we should be more supportive, and Zya pointed out they were all here because they themselves were not getting any, and it's been eighteen months, said Amir to Yaakub, and all Shelley tells me is to wait, no wonder he is up there then, added Khan, he is doing it for his wife and kids. He's doing it for attention, said Yusuf (according to Khalid), he's only going to make it worse for the rest of us because he doesn't know the value of keeping his mouth shut and listening to the authorities. They should be out there soon, said Ahmed, talking to him to get him down. Would that help, asked Zahid, I can just see Robert and Graham and Shelley trying to talk to him from the ground, craning their necks, trying to see him against the sky. Aziz laughed, it would be like looking up at God. Yes, looking up after a very long time, but maybe that is a good thing, him being up there, said Samar, maybe then they will know we really don't want to return. How can they not believe we don't want to return, asked Ahmed, no, it's only processing, he said, but if it is only that then it will only be a matter of time, but Syed (according to Yaakub) in the other building says for him eighteen months is nothing, he is now no longer counting, his number should have been up that long ago, but Syed didn't think to get up there. Maybe now that he has, said Aziz, maybe they will now see what we have not been able to say, but will he be OK up there, wondered Khan, the zinc gets very hot, as hot as our backs when they let us out sometimes, no, hotter than that, yes, yes hotter than that of course, supplied Shiraz, this place, it is like home and it is not like home, they will never make this place like our home, explained Latif, that is why he is up there, standing on zinc and looking down at them.

And the next day, when some of the others, the ones who had been discussing and passing on information, saw him still up there, it was Khalid who predicted this might get bigger. So he isn't just going crazy, said Jamal, no, maybe he has a plan, said Zahid, who was the quiet one but knew him the closest, what plan, has he said anything to you, queried Yusuf, a bit too harshly, thought Zya, as he relayed the update to Syed, yes in here everything is everybody else's business, but we don't need to announce going to the toilet! But this is very far from toilets, said Qamar to Anas later, as the word spread from group to group, language to language, we are all watching, can you see, even though some turn away, like Aziz and Habib and some of the smaller ones shielded by the women, the rest of us, Yaakub pointed out, we're shameless, watching this *tamasha* circus. He's sitting down now, crouched low, look at him, his shirt is drenched, said Salma, in the closest building. Does anyone know what is it he's saying? No, said Sara, he's talking in English, is his English good, wondered Shelley around lunchtime as she walked around the mess, and Zahid almost responded, said Jamal, what a naïve boy, he would've told her his family's in a royal mansion in Afghanistan if asked, poor stupid boy, how would he know, said Yusuf, that it wouldn't help him one bit, that to them we're the poorest of the poor, and need to be to get out?

Someone's here, said Habib, see Shelley rushing outside, you wait here boys, it's all good, she said. They are not in uniform, reported Salma, slightly disappointed, wouldn't they send more uniformed people, I like the kind of blue, makes their eyes even more blue, except you can never say a word properly when they come to you, laughed Aishah, you get so tongue-tied like a sixteen-year-old virgin, not a forty-year-old mother, sshhh, said Salma, trying to deflect her embarrassment, they are talking to Graham and Robert under the roof, OK, OK now, said Shelley, suddenly coming through the building, nothing to see here, she's gone now said Aishah after a while, so what are they doing? They're just talking, said Samad in the other building, you sound disappointed, said Yaakub, did you expect to come and bow down to that great man on the roof, give him salaam and send him on his way? Where did they come from, asked Qamar, did you see out the fences, there is nothing out there. This is a big place, replied Zya, with more gentleness than normal, according to Yusuf, it is still an island, insisted Qamar, which part did they come from? Malik said he didn't see the point. They are defending him, can you not see, they are in clothes I have seen on television, speaking English, they are pointing fingers at Graham, who has his arms crossed. They want to save him, pronounced Aziz. So

141

suddenly the rest had to pause, said Zahid. Yes, see, they are like Americans, Zya reassured Qamar again, I told you, this place is big, Australia, it is very close to America, almost next to it.

Two more, said Khairil, I wonder when did they get up there? I think the question is how did they get up there, said Yusuf (according to Qamar), did they climb up the pipes? I think they're being brave, said Khalid, but, observed Aziz, that only means yesterday's talks didn't work. It cannot work in one day, said Qamar to Zya with big gestures and some pointing. We talked and talked for years before leaving. People come with set agendas, agreed Habib, it would take a long time for one to understand another. Stupid young people, spat Yusuf, they think by making spectacles of themselves they will change the world. Why so negative, *chacha-jaan*, said Zahid, it is better than not knowing what is going to happen any day, how long have you been here? Shut up, you're still a small boy, said Yusuf (when has he ever admitted being wrong, said Zya, even Shelley ignores him now). Speaking of which, said Aziz, I spoke to Salma yesterday, she says Shelley is not telling them anything. They're scared, suggested Qamar, it looks like he's seen things like this before, Khalid pointed out, Qamar thinks the guards are now scared, reported Zya later to Salma in the women's quarters. So many guards scared of three boys on a roof, laughed Salma to Megha. It is not what they're doing, it's why they're doing it, said Megha, my cousin, the one in Quetta, told me the white people don't react much to just saying the truth, but they react when it is shown, when it is not hidden but seen. I had told him then he fancied himself an American, and then, said Sara, she went silent, just like we all do after speaking of the ones far away. She has been waiting long, said

Aishah, she has been here from the time I came, how far are you in the queue, asked Amena, does it matter, Salma sighed, I am losing count, those boys are trying to jump the queue, said Sara, sshh, do you want Shelley to hear, said Amena, maybe they will talk for all of us, said Salma, no, impossible, Aishah refuted, Qamar said they're having trouble communicating. That's because it's just those guards and those people who came in from outside, said Salma (and Aishah later relayed to Qamar to tell the men) if the Americans (Australians, corrected Amena) like all the showing, then we must do more showing. Keep the showing, keep the show going, how do they say it, asked Salma, the show must go on, replied Amena.

No, guys, sorry, not today, said Shelley, are there any more up on the roof, asked Rizwan, no, replied Aziz, but I don't think that's the reason why we aren't going out today, it's the cameras, said Zahid, they don't want us captured on it, can you see how many asked Yusuf (was his voice trembling then, queried Zya later), about five six, but they are big, said Jamal, how would you know, you seen film shooting before, asked Yaakub, Amitabh Bachchan came to Afghanistan, retorted Jamal, I was ten years old, they had very big cameras. Aziz told Khairil later he felt Jamal was lying, that he was making it up, let it be, Khairil replied, they put him in that tiny dark room for too long, he's been telling tales ever since he came out. Nothing to do but nod and say yes and hope the boys on the roof somehow do something soon enough that we all don't end up the same. There are people on mikes now, pointed Habib, you can see them from this window. What are they saying, asked Yusuf, Qamar should be here, he could translate, well it's all about the boys anyway, noted Jamal, they are the ones everyone can see. They will put this on television, said Habib, then all of them will be famous, people will know about us and release us. They won't, not that quickly, said Yusuf, what is wrong with you, do you not want to continue what has been interrupted, roared Khairil, it will not do the boys good if we fight, said Aziz, we must keep calm, the boys are doing their best. They've crouched now, said Zya, they're darker with the sun. They must be hungry, said Faisal, apparently they asked for water earlier, reported Yaakub, Shelley was very angry about that, she was slamming doors again. She was angry that they asked? enquired Yusuf, no, you know Shelley tries, she looks at you directly and she tells you to your face. Maybe she was angry with the other guards, wondered Jamal. Maybe we should ask her what is going on, said Habib. Now its twelve people talking to three boys, observed Zahid, they must be taking this seriously. You really think this would make a difference, asked Yusuf, oh, *chacha-jaan*, Zahid replied, this is the most exciting thing that has happened since I came here, I don't know about you, but I think the Australians outside are not like these guards, but more like Shelley. That's why the cameras are here, agreed Jamal, the cameras mean other people outside know, and that will make us processed faster. Don't think I'm an idiot, said Yusuf (according to Zya, talking to Qamar). I know how it all works. We must keep calm, repeated Aziz. You keep calm, said Zahid, while they put their life up there. One bullet, yes, agreed Habib, and its finished. But not while the cameras are here, said Zahid softly. I really want Qamar here, said Khairil.

Are you still counting, asked Salma, it takes a while from here, be patient, said Amena. Eight, said Megha decisively. Your banner is looking really good, Salma, said Sara, it's nothing said Salma, oh so modest, teased Amena. It only took me an hour, continued Salma (she's so proud of it, said Sara to Qamar). Did you see Shelley's face when the boys unfurled it, asked Aishah, I think she might've smiled, Shelley smile! exclaimed Salma, what are you saying? Qamar said the cameras focused on it a lot, from where he stood, continued Sara.

More boys, not eating, it is like they are now young Gandhis, said Megha. The new ones up there, how long have they been here, asked Aishah. I don't think they're Hazaras, the new ones, said Sara. Whoever they are, said Salma, they have strength, look at them. Their mothers aren't here, which is probably a good thing, said Megha, yes, although, said Khatija, I'm sure they miss them, they must be thinking of them as they sleep on those terrible tiles. Yes, Megha and Aishah nodded, it is not easy what they're doing, they must have been pushed to some crazy point. Boys take these things harder, said Salma to nobody in particular, is Afzal okay, she asked Aishah (was it necessary to bring that up right then, Khatija complained to Sara) yes he is, said Aishah, he is sleeping, he was very tired afterwards. At least Shelley let you have him, said Salma, if it had been one of the others, they would've left it after bandaging his wrists. Shelley knows he's nine, said Aishah, the others probably didn't ask, you don't need words to know a boy's age, said Amena (you're right, but don't scare her, said Salma to her later), there is no blame here, said Megha, oh but there is so much blame, Megha, said Amena, that I don't know where to start. The cameras are now all around, said Salma, the news must be growing big, does that mean the guards will listen to the boys, asked Sara, it's so frustrating that we don't know what they're saying.

Nobody has responded to our newspaper request yet, said Amena. I don't think they will let us have newspapers, said Aishah, maybe that's a good sign, said Megha. There are more people now, said Salma, just standing around from outside the fence and watching. The boys are now famous, said Aishah, Allah protect them, they give me strength. We are not going outside today either, said Megha, I think Shelley has been given strict orders. That's okay, said Salma, Qamar said he heard some reporters talk to their cameras using the newspaper words. It's how they see us, shrugged Sara, as long as it gets us out. Do the boys know what to say to get us out, though, asked Aishah, of course, there's so many of them now, said Sara, they will speak for all of us, in here we are the same. I am going to work as a banker when I get out, said Megha (always with her plans, that Megha, said Salma to Aishah), I want to deal with a lot of money. Fool and money soon parted, said Amena, it's an English saying, wah wah, Amena madam, said Sara, maybe you will become English teacher. Of course not, said Amena, I will work in the newspapers, like those people, I will write about all the bad things happening in the world. And you will also write about all the things I sew and knit, said Salma, of course, I will write about everything. I will bring Mahdi over, said Sara, and my son will go to school here. School in America (Australia, said Amena) will be very expensive, said Salma, no, Khairil said it is free, he heard Shelly say so, said Sara. You must tell that to your son Afzal, said Salma to Aishah, he must know what to expect out there. Yes, agreed Aishah, there is so much to prepare.

He's asking for water, said Zya (according to Khalid). He had bent down and asked Graham. Did they give him any, asked Yusuf, no, I don't know, I don't think so, said

Qamar. Did anyone go to talk to them, asked Zahid, we were out for a bit yesterday, the first boy just keeps saying they will not eat till they are free, informed Jamal. He's saying that even when Graham is on the megaphone asking them all to come down, saying they will hurt themselves, said Zya, oh, suddenly our safety is so important, laughed Aziz, yes, because it is all being captured on camera, who knows what has been on television, wondered Qamar, I haven't seen television in months, wouldn't it be funny, that we come here and the first real thing that happens is we end up on white man television, Yaakub pointed out, and it was such an absurd thought that everyone laughed, relayed Habib to Aishah, and it was odd that we did with everything happening outside, oh not at all, replied Aishah, I think it's necessary, we need it, it's a good relief, even if its temporary, besides we shouldn't let those boys down. We're not really eating either, Khairil observed absently, as if, said Jamal, he was trying to make conversation about safer things but only making it worse, Latif said this made him feel closer to the boys, even though he wasn't burning his feet on the roof with them, they could've at least taken their shoes up there, mused Salma, it would've not lasted, said Amena, and anyway I don't see how that is important when they are all still out there, what is this a standstill, enquired Fatima, nobody seems to be doing anything, one of them used to get visits from an uncle, noted Aishah (but we all know that, Zya told her later) have they gone to get him maybe, I doubt it, I don't see Yara anymore, said Amena, I haven't seen her for two months, maybe she came but wasn't allowed in, suggested Salma (as usual, with her complete lack of tact, what good does it do, complained Aishah to Jamal), the boys must be missing their mothers, said Latifah, holding Aishah's Afzal, noted Amena, as if he were her own, they must be very scared, they probably never thought this would go on for so long, what's worse is if they were thinking they should've done it earlier, noted Hafiz, if they had known what kind of attention it would get, rather than wasting time listening to Shelley, said Khairil, well that's because there's such a thing as faith, said Yusuf, faith that is more than just touching your head to the floor five times a day. And your faith is that by keeping silent and licking their asses they will let you out, *chacha-jaan*, asked Yaakub (according to Zya), some courtesy towards the elders, observed Salma, it is already going, being on this American land (Australian, sighed Amena), am I the only one who understands the nature of this place, said Yusuf, where things like law and order actually exist and isn't a figment of a corrupt politician's imagination (I understand, said Hafiz), this is only another reaction to being here, isn't it, suggested Salma when she heard of it, some things are as big, too big, to understand, so the logical reaction is to believe it is also better, he really believes it doesn't he, poor *chacha-jaan*, said Aishah softly, after putting Afzal to sleep, I think he believes we should be grateful, said Sharifah, that we're here at all, we have already been that, interrupted Amena, those boys aren't up there for fun, it's not like they are unfaithful kafirs, Yusuf *chacha* should have some empathy, he didn't mean to disrespect them, Amena, said Salma, he is of the same ilk as my in-laws back home, who survived generations by hiding themselves, it's not cowardice, it's a different kind of courage, this kind of stuff is probably scaring him silly, if so then maybe he doesn't deserve to get out (oh, Amena, sighed Aishah) because he is only going to be the same out there, hiding away from everything, if that's the way his family has been for years, finished Amena, and Qamar said for some hours nobody talked to her, because they had all been so intent on the boys and getting out but nobody had really thought about what that would be like, and isn't that just like them, ventured Latif, saying so many things they shouldn't, even the honest ones, but it's something to be said that they were all quiet about it, because, you know, Zahid said, hedging and hesitant, the truth is, we will do anything, like these boys, to get out, but who knows what out *is*, well then we must believe Yusuf is right, felt Jamal, that it is a place of law and order, but, Khairil contradicted, if they don't like us in here, they may not like us out there, oh you're saying that from all the poison your cousin outside says on visits, said Habib, it is only about what to prepare for, Habib, said Zya, but no, no, said Habib, I don't want to think about it that way.

And while the boys still fasted up on the roof, with everyone, even Shelley, watching and anticipating more, Amena said all of a sudden it meant nothing that they were up there, and that she was going to ask for something to eat, I told you she would go crazy, because like Jamal one day, said Zya, no, she had had a surprise visit from her cousin Yara, said Qamar, everyone is watching the television, the boys are everywhere, ah but that is good news, said Zahid, maybe tomorrow I will ask Shelley again about my file, ask all you want, Yara said we are going to be sent back (what, Khalid, what do you mean, asked Yusuf), the big government people want to stop the boat owners from coming here, but we are already here, Aziz pointed out, are they going to put us back on the boats, you are lying, that girl must have it wrong, said Salma, maybe her English isn't very good and she misunderstood, said Qamar with hope (all we have left, said Jamal to Habib). But what if it's true, oh get the boys to come down then, let them eat, said Aishah, already thinking of Afzal, have you seen them now, their faces are completely different, not like when they first went up, said Khatijah, I don't know, I feel like I've been seeing them like this for so long I no longer remember what they were like before, said Salma, how odd, even Zahid said that, mentioned Yaakub, and he was on the same boat as them. I am now afraid they *will* get processed faster, how awful, said Fatima, bursting into tears, can you imagine if they get out there and nobody gives them a job, oh get a hold of yourself, it is not like that, anyway so many relatives are here, it must be for a reason, said Yaakub (but I don't think he really believed it, observed Farhan). We're still going to be up here, they've reported to have said, and maybe they already knew what outside was like, said Zya, they're losing weight, said Salma, I swear I saw one close his eyes for a while, he probably fainted but didn't want anyone to know, do they really hate us so much, Aishah asked suddenly, and Fatima was certain she had been thinking of Afzal's bandages, in all the rooftop attention nobody had thought of changing the dressing, she is as vulnerable as those boys, pronounced Khairil, she must feel a special connection to them. Do we have a choice in this, Yusuf spoke up unexpectedly, let them hate us, let them think what they want, here, there, what does it matter, I will still go out there to live, and with that Yusuf (according to Zya) seemed to be done talking about the whole issue, and it really seemed rather appropriate that in this way Yusuf *chacha-jaan* had articulated the most honest truth of all, the truth which had bound them on boats then and on rooftops now.

None of them was reported to look very good, which

was the answer everyone received when they asked, and it was always the first question of the morning. They aren't giving us water, the youngest was reported to have said, we've asked but they said we'll get it if we come down, are the press covering this, asked Salma, we must find a way to get something positive out of this situation, stressed Amena, the law is still the law, said Shelley later on, suddenly, it seemed, to be on talking terms again, as if the implication of her true loyalty in those days of silence hadn't existed, she's only doing her job, defended Yusuf, I'm surprised people still listen to him, said Amena. The first boy refused the compromise because it came too late, said Khairil, I think I overheard that lady with the mike say they will look at our files again, how many times are they going to look at the files, nothing has changed inside it, said Yaakub, Aishah brought Afzal out last night, to show his bandages to the cameras, said Jamal, and Habib was a little concerned about his tone, since it seemed cloudier than usual, she wanted them to see what was happening, what her boy had done to himself. Now, now, no such talk here, said Shelley, coming in, although she could not meet Jamal's eyes, according to Khalid, and she later brought them all some chocolate, which Aziz flung against the wall. Afzal might want that, said Qamar, just make sure the boys don't hear of it, they might think us unworthy of what they're fighting for, scrambling like beggars while they waste away like patients with a disease, nobody wanting to touch them. Some of the names have been called, according to Sara, only a sham a part of the so-called compromise, sneered Amena, still, we must take what is offered, otherwise we insult the efforts of the boys, said Khatija, and most of the women nodded, although Qamar expressed a certain dissatisfaction with how easily everyone changed their minds, isn't that also being really selfish and disrespectful, he told Ishan, who then told Amena, what kind of signal does that send out about us, and the women agreed what nobody else saw was how the atmosphere had changed, there was no longer that dense layer of bodies at the outer fence plastering against it and shouting slogans, and the number of mikes and questions had slowed from a torrent to a trickle, and Amena was just slightly annoyed that people might start saying Yusuf was right after all, especially since showing Afzal seemed to have attracted not enough attention. The funny thing is, said Jamal, if we were Christian this wouldn't be the case, and Habib and Aziz tried weak protests, buts its true, insisted Jamal, the guards used to let them out every week to go out to the Church, and they would attend service and return, while waiting to be processed, and they would ask for eggs, because they missed them, if only they could bring some back for us, this is hardly the time, interjected Khairil, but you cannot deny it, Jamal went on, and maybe instead of punishing themselves like this, what the boys need to do is to convert into Christianity, and we should too, no, no, please hear me out, I'm not being insensitive, I'm not saying do it literally, but in name, the white man is all about appearances, if we appear to be Christian, but still remain what we are inside, they will let us out faster, we can do this, I remember Christians in Iran, they would hide and pray to Jesus, but go to mosque on Fridays, so people would leave them alone. And just as Aziz and Qamar and even Yusuf cocked their ears to this, Jamal continued, and I would follow them home, and I would ask them why they are so afraid, and they would say sir, you do not know what we go through, and I said look, it is only what is in your heart that matters, don't worry about what others say, not even me, oh sir, they said, thank you for saying this to us, it is wise indeed, and they gave me a big hug, and this is where Jamal lost them. Let it be, said Khairil to Habib, there is no use telling him he's lying, he doesn't see it that way. It's the result of Red One, said Qamar, when you've been in there too long too young, I hope they don't put the boys in there, said Khalid, it might be too late for everyone, was Yusuf's solemn thought (don't say that, *chacha-jaan*, said Khairil) but this is what we're coming to, sitting around babbling nonsense, I wonder who is worse off, the boys or us.

Sara saw Salma out there with them when they came down, reported Qamar. She said they did not speak much, as if all the words they had were already exhausted, and there was nothing left. They didn't even correct her when she told them this was the nature of America, according to Amena. They did smile at her as the guards took them away, if she's to be believed, said Khairil, it's not Red One, please tell me it's not Red One, was Aziz's worry, no, if you put eight boys in a single room, the room loses its purpose, Jamal pointed out (very fittingly, surmised Khalid). Do they know about their files, asked Fatima, maybe they're being processed right now, Amena has already gathered all the women's files, said Qamar, just to be on the safe side, yes, we should do the same, felt Habib, but what do we tell Shelley, why, the truth, shrugged Khairil, as if this happened every day, our stages are different but we want the same thing, and the mention of it opened the thing none of them could say while the boys were on the roof, all their stages, levels, checks, what's done, what's left, my bones are in those files, said Jamal, and oddly nobody, not even Amena, thought that as crazy. When

Salma came back Aishah rushed to her, because, according to Latifah, she knew beforehand a collapse was imminent, and sure enough, there were her cries, ululating off the walls, it's like they're mine, she said (strength, said Aishah, strength, sister) all I did was pass some water into their lips, so swollen, so cracked, she said, as if describing a painting or a distant memory, they looked at me but did not seem to recognise me, but of course they know you, they're just in shock, said Aishah, but Salma wasn't listening, felt Sara, because she could finally release herself and she wasn't going to have it stymied. How far has she been processed, asked Shelley, watching from a doorway (oh what a fright that was, whispered Sara to Khatija) and Amena lied, according to Qamar, because this had already happened, everyone knew each other's stages, it is envy that isn't in our control, agreed Khairil, we don't determine the dates, and it is what put them up there in the first place, said Zya, this fear of being left behind as others race to the outside. We're going in reverse, said Habib, it's like we're becoming children again, and have to relearn everything, but Zahid disagreed, having been to the boys himself, felt they had aged, as if they had encountered something none of them had seen and were in a strange state, almost as if in peace. *Astafaullah-al-azim*, said Aishah when she heard, after putting both Afzal and Salma to sleep, he blasphemes, no, he's trying to keep things stable, said Amena with an air of finality. Latif asked if the boys recognised Zahid, and according to Zya one of them may have, because when he caught sight of him, in between gulping some water and eyeing some sandwiches, he smiled, and brazenly asked Zahid to tell him a story. Aishah was certain Zahid had misheard, it seemed such an unusual thing to say, but what is usual about this, asked Qamar, we are all stories for the camera and the chanting people outside, they are only asking to be fed, and Jamal laughed so loud Sara said it woke Salma up, she said it must have travelled across all those lines of people, they must be hungry, said Qamar, they must be very very hungry.